MAISY'S MIRROR

Cover design by The Killion Group
http://thekilliongroupinc.com

MAISY'S MIRROR

Mimi Foster

MIMI FOSTER

All the best

Mimi Foster

 ONE

March 1916

"There's a delivery for you, Mrs. Raines."

"What is it, Janet?"

"I have no idea, ma'am. Two men brought a crate to the door and said it was for you. I had them leave it in the foyer. This letter was with it."

The box was almost as tall as she. "Will you have Mr. Rosco bring the necessary tools to unpack it, please?"

"Of course, ma'am."

The note was from her dear husband: 'Its beauty reminded me of your radiance which is apparent to all but you. When you reflect on your image, remember how much you are loved.'

She had Mr. Rosco hang the exquisite mirror in a place of honor in the parlor so she could admire it every day.

March 2016

Margaret kept her face expressionless as the slightly overweight, middle-aged woman approached.

1

"He's a beauty, isn't he?"

The slight lift of an eyebrow was apparently the only encouragement the chatty proprietress needed to continue with her monologue.

"It's been in my husband's family for decades and I've always thought of it as 'he.' Not sure why with all its fancy scrolls and doo-dads."

Margaret had been dismayed as she'd passed the crisp white bungalow on her way home from her afternoon walk that she took like clockwork at two-thirty each day. An attractive young widow in her late-twenties, she had worked hard to avoid unnecessary encounters with the locals in the two years since she'd arrived in this quaint village on the New England shoreline.

A recent gale had felled a massive elm across her customary secluded trail. Too high to climb over, too long to go around without navigating the brambles, she had opted to take this sparsely populated road that would lead to the front of her house instead of the back, more scenic route.

She wanted to keep to her typical, uncommunicative self as she passed the Estate Sale being held on the well-manicured lawn, but sunrays peeking through gathering clouds gleamed off the ornate mirror and caught her attention. The mirror called to her like a siren's song, causing a tightening in her chest and a rush of adrenalin. Crossing the street pulled her from her comfort zone, but she needed to see if it was as alluring as it appeared from a distance.

Her breath caught as she approached. Not at all in keeping with her normal no-nonsense, no-frill style, she would pay whatever was necessary to own it, but dreaded the inevitable encounter she would have to go through to make the item hers.

She had pushed herself to the point of pain on today's walk. Feathery strands of chocolate brown hair escaped the strict confines of her ponytail, and sweat adhered her sheer blouse to her back in the muggy stillness. She was sticky and uncomfortable, and even more desirous of being alone than usual.

"How much?" She didn't want to engage in conversation, she just wanted to make her purchase and escape.

"There's a doozie of a storm rolling in and I was just getting ready to close up shop, so I'll let you have him for half price – one fifty."

She continued to stare at the impressive mirror, her well-trained features showing no hint of movement, hoping her bubbling excitement wasn't evident.

The gabby woman was not a salesperson and should have stopped while she was ahead. Margaret would have paid full price without a second thought.

"Tell you what. Make it one hundred and I'll give you a ride home."

"That won't be necessary, but thank you, I'll take it. I don't have cash with me. May I come back to pick it up?"

The first warm drops of a late spring shower struck her face as the woman hefted the mirror and rested it on a blanket in the back of her truck. "Jonathan! Come take this stuff in! It's gonna come a cropper!"

A tall, thin man hurried out of the garage with a friendly wave. "I'll bring the rest inside. You do what you need to." The pelting droplets plunged closer and faster.

"Hop in. We don't have much time," she shouted above the rising wind.

Arguing would be futile. She had to lift herself on

3

tiptoe to get the proper angle to pull the heavy truck door open. Stepping into the high-rise of the cab caused her to wince as pain shot up her leg. "My house is . . ."

"I know where you live. Donovan, the man you bought your place from, is my husband's brother, twin actually. House has been in their family not quite as long as your mirror, but pretty close."

The words flowed over deaf ears because she didn't remember much about the time when she'd moved here, so it was no surprise that she knew nothing of the seller. Her desire to be isolated and avoid human contact led her to this remote area, and being trapped in a confined space with a talkative stranger was the embodiment of her worst nightmares.

"I'm sorry your leg is still giving you trouble. We were all hoping your daily walks would get you healthy and clear away some of the gloom of losing your husband."

Margaret took a deep breath to control her ire, holding her hands together so the driver wouldn't notice her anger. How dare she presume to know about her accident, her recovery, or anything else about her life?

"Don't go getting your feathers ruffled. You keep to yourself, but everyone knows everyone else's business. It's what happens in a small town."

This woman didn't have a clue about her, but she wouldn't be perverse and point that out. The ride down the tranquil street was anything but, and seemed more like ten miles than the half mile it actually was.

"We own a little house about an hour up the road in Bangor. We're getting too old to stay on the Bay year round, so Jonathan's nephew is going to buy our place. Keep it in the family. I'm Sarah, by the way."

Margaret wasn't paying attention. Being enclosed in a

car with a chattering busybody had her feeling like her skin was shrinking.

"We'll be around a few more weeks, maybe more. Jonathan's nephew loves to travel the world, so I'm not sure when he'll be here, but he plans on sometime next spring. The house will be vacant until then, but we'll come occasionally to check on it. Oh, to be young and single again, huh?"

The pounding rain sounded like bullets on the roof of the truck, and combined with the rapid staccato thump of the wiper blades, many of Sarah's words were thankfully drowned out.

Not getting a response, she continued to share information Margaret wasn't interested in. "Got a lot to get rid of to move into a pint-sized place after we've spent decades here. Don't understand how we've accumulated so much stuff. How did you end up in Castine?"

They pulled into the drive and Margaret opened the hefty door, ignoring the question. At five foot two, the ground was a long way down as she slid out of the truck into a puddle of muddy water, making sure her good leg took the impact.

"I'll get the mirror, it's heavy," Sarah said.

"No!" She hadn't meant to be abrupt but she didn't want anyone intruding on her sanctuary. "Sorry, but I can take care of it. You stay here. I'll be right out."

"It's no trouble at all." She reached for the handle.

"Please," Margaret said, meeting the woman's eyes. "Stay here."

She didn't care if this friendly meddler thought she had bodies hidden in her house, she treasured her privacy and wouldn't let this long-winded Good Samaritan invade it.

"Thank you," she whispered as the lady sat back in her seat. "I'll be right out."

Raindrops spewed furiously as she lifted the mirror to the ground and latched the tailgate. The woman had not been wrong, but pride wouldn't allow Margaret to show even a slight indication of its heaviness as she hurried through bombarding beads of water.

Reaching the front porch, she leaned her new purchase against the pale green lapboard siding as she wrestled to pull keys from her sodden pocket. She struggled to move her new asset the final few feet into the house, then rushed to retrieve the cash to send her neighbor on her way.

Without the weight of the mirror and the need for protection, she approached the truck at a slower speed, enjoying the drenching downpour as water from the rain got in her eyes, making her smile. Sarah rolled the window down slightly as Margaret squinted and handed over the money.

"We'll be around for a while," she said above the noise. "You holler if you need anything. As a matter of fact, Jonathan can come hang your mirror . . ."

"No, thank you. I'm quite capable. Thank you for your generosity," she called over her shoulder, not caring whether Sarah heard her as she headed through what was now a deluge.

She leaned against the closed door, strands of hair that had escaped her ponytail matted to her face, shirt now transparent and plastered to her torso, pants and shoes dripping wet. She wondered why people like Sarah thought they knew you before you'd even met?

Sarah and the other townspeople could only guess about the car accident that had killed her husband and left her almost crippled. They didn't understand what it was about their little town that called to her soul, or why she coveted her solitude. They were all strangers who only knew what they fancied as truth. But that was their problem, not hers.

She looked around her cozy cottage and shook off her sour mood in exchange for the elation streaming through her as the proud owner of the magnificent mirror. There wasn't anything in her home that didn't bring her pleasure, and this would be the masterpiece. The river rock hearth extended along the right wall and was interrupted only by the oversized fireplace situated in the middle.

Margaret stripped out of her waterlogged clothes. Walking naked through her living room and kitchen with an armful of dripping clothes cocooned in the entryway rug, she started a load of laundry. The next batch would include her tennis shoes and the rug, but in the meantime a warm shower beckoned.

Long-dormant excitement welled as she dried off her thin frame. She beamed as she studied her recent acquisition. Changing into comfortable clothes, she knew exactly where she would hang it. Gathering tools from her garage, she lifted the mirror with sheer determination.

With one foot on her desk and one on the ladder, she prepared to drill a pilot hole but was sidetracked thinking if she hung it on the adjacent wall, there would be a constant reflection of Penobscot Bay and the waves that empowered her. She was pleased with her cleverness and went about doing what needed to be done.

The process took longer than expected, but when it was precisely placed and she admired her handiwork, energy like she hadn't experienced in months buoyed her. No matter which way she turned, her picture perfect scene was part of the room, and there was a pronounced difference in her surroundings. The mirror was a brilliant find.

"Why are you crying?"

The deep, masculine voice sounded like it was nearby. Margaret sat up from her well-used spot on the couch that had absorbed more tears over the past two years than she could imagine. Heart pounding, she searched the empty room. Nothing was out of place and there was no sign of an intruder. She didn't know what had disturbed her, but she grinned when she considered she was well and truly losing her mind in her solitary existence in her refuge by the sea.

Each year her seclusion wedged a little more distance between herself and civilization, from the people she had called family and the friends she'd known her whole life. She would make a conscious effort this summer to get out more. Not to meet people, but to reacquaint herself occasionally with life outside of this shelter.

"Why are you forlorn? I've got nowhere else to be if you'd like to talk."

Rising slowly, only her eyes traveling the room, she asked in almost a whisper, "Who's there?"

Silence.

"Hello? Is someone here?"

With her back to the wall, she inched her way to the bedroom and removed the revolver from the nightstand, her eyes drawn away from her surroundings only long enough to assure herself her gun was loaded and ready. Slowly searching each room and closet of the house, her bare feet silent on the polished wooden floors, she checked doors and windows to make sure she hadn't somehow gotten slack and left something unlocked. Confident there was no trespasser, she relaxed as she returned her trusty defense weapon to the otherwise-empty drawer of her modern, black bedside table.

The rumbling of her stomach alerted her to how long it had been since she'd eaten. She chalked up the unusual voice to the muddled effects of hunger. Either that or her self-imposed exile had made her mad as a hatter.

Out her window her path to the sea was strewn with freshly budded spring leaves from the afternoon storm. She drew the heavy curtains closed against the dusk and made dinner. Tomorrow she'd return to her writing and stop this cycle of loneliness that appeared to be threatening her sanity. She'd been too long without company and now she was hearing voices. Maybe her mother was right about the effects of isolation, but she wasn't ready to face that possibility.

The welcoming rays of sun lit the morning sky and snuck through and around the small openings of her curtains. Coffee percolated as she reveled in the warmth of her shower.

Pouring her first cup of the day, she retrieved her notes and relaxed in her office, looking around the sparsely furnished but well-appointed room that brought her tranquility. Each room in her small home was decorated with only colors, furniture, and adornments that encouraged pleasure or peace in her. Nothing was out of place and everything had its purpose.

She'd been dragging her feet, and while her direction with the novel she was writing still wasn't clear, this morning there was a renewed sense of motivation as she stared at the imposing mirror above her desk as though it might give her the words she needed to write a story she had no interest in telling.

Maybe she could salvage this book after all and get on to a proposal she'd find more engaging. The spring morning shining into her space was crisp, and she opened her computer, resolved to complete several chapters to send to her agent.

Her publisher had given her a substantial advance before the accident and hadn't pressed her for a long time afterward so she could get back on her feet, figuratively and literally. If she didn't have something of substance soon, she'd have to return the money. The time had come to pay the piper.

Even with her new intensity, her writing didn't hold her attention for long. She found herself pacing, walking the same path on the timeless rug with the vintage pattern she'd walked in this room a hundred times before. The shooting pain in her leg kept the memory of that fateful night alive. She would never be free of the sounds, the sights, the horror.

But she was never guilty. She refused. Reaction brewed. She wanted to channel it, express it, wanted to let go of it once and for all, but anger always took its place, and she would get no further than she had the day before.

"You'll regret it if you throw it."

She whirled to face an unoccupied room. "Who's there?"

"You'll lose your favorite cup if you smash it." It was the polished male voice she'd heard before, but since it wasn't real it hardly mattered.

She rinsed her red mug in the kitchen sink, somehow

sad she'd finally snapped. "Thank you, you're right. It is special to me."

Nothing. No reply.

"Is someone here?"

Silence.

"Hearing voices, talking to myself. That sounds about right."

Fixing another cup of coffee, she wandered back to her desk and studied the mirror. The morning sun coming through the windows shined on the crystal bowl of lemons and lavender that she kept there. Feeling the draw and inspiration from her new purchase, she was determined to channel the excitement she found. Beginning yet again, her fingers flew over the keyboard with purpose as emotions focused on the story she was supposed to be telling.

Probably original to the house, the small brass antique hook by the front door in the shape of an Irish Setter was the perfect place to hang her keys after her ritual two-point-two-mile walk she had prescribed for herself so many months ago. Each day her efforts became a little easier, but today she was eager to be home in her bright cottage, motivated for a change, not having a clue what was simmering inside her.

She had to have a work in progress to her agent, sooner rather than later. Every day she applied herself to the task at hand but never made much headway. If the topic and storyline didn't interest her, how was it going to interest anyone else?

The blank screen screamed at her, convincing her she was a fraud, encouraging her belief she'd never be able to write again. Was there another bestseller in her, or was she fooling them and herself? She was skating on thin ice with her editor and agent, and this might be the last time Jonnell would put her neck on the line for her.

"There's no need for despair," the man's voice said softly. After the initial rush of adrenalin, Margaret took a cleansing breath to still her frazzled nerves and wonder at the new twist her brain was taking.

"Who are you?" she asked, proud of how calm her voice sounded. Did it make her more sane or more crazy that she asked such a question to the empty room?

"William." The voice was deep but pleasant, friendly but somehow reserved.

"Are you a figment of my imagination, William?"

"You're not crazy, if that's what you're asking, just slightly wounded."

She stood abruptly and stepped to her peaceful kitchen. Even her imaginary friend wanted to talk about her injuries.

"I wasn't referring to your leg, I meant your spirit. You need encouragement, not all of this time by yourself, thoughts wrestling each other to exhaustion with no objective voice to help pull you away from the ledge."

Her bark of laughter was immediate. "Right. A random voice in my head is going to pull me back to sanity. Thanks, Wills."

Silence.

"You don't mind if I call you 'Wills,' do you? After all, if I'm going to be talking to someone in an empty room who doesn't exist, I might as well call you something less formal."

"Something less formal like 'Margaret'?" There was amusement in his voice. "I think that's fair. I rather like 'Wills.' It's personal and friendly."

"Well, that's a relief."

"I beg your pardon?"

"Never mind."

"Oh, I see. I'm being treated to your sarcasm. I enjoy it."

Her frown etched deep lines between her brows as she looked around the empty room, shaking her head.

"You won't mind if I call you 'Maisy' then, will you?"

So their conversation was to continue. She considered his words for a moment. To almost everyone in her life she'd been Margaret. Occasionally Meggie, rarely Magnolia, but mostly Margaret. "I think I like it. No one's ever called me that before." With a nod she said, "Wills and Maisy it is." She opened the door to her vintage refrigerator to find something to eat. "Can I fix you lunch, Wills?"

"I don't eat, but thank you for the offer."

"You don't eat?" She stood, holding the door open, looking around the room. She was alone, but the thought of having someone to talk to was kind of intriguing . . . and dangerous. She'd never considered that being a recluse would make her senseless.

"That's good to know. How do you sustain yourself?"

The baritone rumble came from deep in his nonexistent chest. "I manage."

She melted cheese on a tortilla and fixed herself a salad.

"May I ask what that is?"

"My quesadilla?" she asked, holding it up.

"No, the machine you put it in. It came out hot, but I'm not familiar with the appliance."

"The microwave?" The lines between her brows deepened.

"I suppose. Is it a cooker of some kind?"

"Yes, it's a super-fast oven of sorts. Are you pulling my leg?"

She sat at her pristine yellow table in her pristine yellow kitchen, eating the simple lunch she'd prepared, and considered this bizarre turn of events. She felt foolish for her sense of panic when he didn't respond. Would he disappear if she wasn't talking to him?

Deciding to change tacks, she said, "Where do you live, Wills?"

"Here."

"Here?" she parroted. "As in 'here' in my house?"

"Well, before it was your house, it was my house."

The fork stopped halfway to her mouth.

"Cat got your tongue?" he asked.

"Just trying to filter your insistence that you live here and measure it against what degree of crazy I've fallen into. Like Alice falling down the rabbit hole."

"Lewis Carroll? I remember reading him in grade school."

Something about the vague way he mentioned it made her ask, "And when was that?"

"Nineteen-twenty-five, twenty-six, sometime around then."

She set her fork down, eyes closing, head leaning forward. "Just for the sake of asking, how old were you?"

"Let's see. I was in third grade, so I must have been seven or eight."

She took her plate to the sink, swiped what was left into the disposal, and stepped out the back door to her familiar path. There was a soft breeze blowing across the water and the sun was low in the sky. A brilliant orange blazed over the landscape as she made her way in the opposite direction of her normal trail on the ridge above the Bay. She walked and walked, then walked some more, enjoying the sound of crunching pine needles and the smell that reminded her of citrus.

The pain in her leg refocused her to the surroundings and an awareness that the sun had set. The tide had come in, and she was further up the path than she'd been in a while, especially in the dark.

She wasn't concerned as she approached her shadowy cottage. She rarely had lights on during the day, and she hadn't expected to be gone this long. She locked the door behind her as she switched on the charming kitchen light, casting a warm golden glow over the table. Everything was as it had been when she left.

She put on soft pajamas after drying off from her hot shower, and did her nightly routine of closing curtains and checking doors and windows. Standing in the shadows admiring her new mirror, she vowed to herself that tomorrow she would buckle down and work on her manuscript in earnest.

"Are you still here, Wills?"

No reply. What could she hold on to to keep her mental balance? She snuggled under the covers and turned off the bedside lamp. Softly she said, "Goodnight, Wills."

She was disappointed at the silence, but also relieved that maybe her walk had cleared her head. She didn't have a clue what her earlier conversation had been about, but she didn't seem to be certifiable yet. She went to sleep dreaming of a young boy in knickers at a wooden desk reading *Alice In Wonderland*, and wondering where he was now.

"Yes, Jonnell, I've been working. You'll have something soon."

Margaret rolled her eyes as she listened to the same lecture she'd heard dozens of times from her agent about passion and focus and deadlines and making her work a priority. She hadn't been able to settle down since the day she'd had the strange encounter with the imaginary Wills, always waiting for – she wasn't sure what.

"Yes, I understand. I didn't have internet connection."

She rubbed a hand down her face and took a deep breath to stay calm as she listened to the raised voice on the other end. "Of course I'm not making that up . . . yes, it's up and running again."

Maybe if she dictated a story while she paced? Her thoughts were more organized walking the same path in her confined space. But she knew she'd still be uninspired.

"Yes, I'll send you what I have by the weekend. Sure. Bye."

The pen she held became a projectile and there was mild satisfaction as the pieces shattered across the gleaming oak floor. She threw herself on the couch, tears wetting her sleeve as she let loose with pent up emotion and frustration, shoulders shaking, cheek resting on her forearm.

"Why are you crying, Maisy?" His voice was gentle, concerned.

"Wills?" She sniffed, sitting up, wiping her cheeks.

"You thought maybe someone else was here?"

"No, but I don't think you're here either, so it hardly matters." She got up and traced her usual path across the living room.

"What has you troubled? And who is Jonnell that she upsets you so?"

"My agent. I'm supposed to have *anything* from my next book to her this weekend, and I can't concentrate long enough to produce diddly-squat."

"What's the story about?"

"It's been so long, I'm not sure I still have a grasp of the original idea. The premise is about best friends who fall in love with the same guy, but I'm not interested in writing it anymore. Jonnell wants something soon."

"Would you like someone to bounce ideas off? I'm a good listener."

"You're not even real, why would I tell you what even I don't understand?"

"Because you need someone to talk to."

"So I've made you up to be my sounding board, is that it?"

"Is that what I said?"

"No, but it's my take away. I'm going to hold myself together and finish something, anything. All I have to do is concentrate."

But her thoughts wouldn't form long enough to convert to the keyboard, and an hour later when she had written no more than a hundred words, she slammed the door in frustration as she set out early for her daily trek.

She knew what she wanted to write, knew she could make a good story, and the ideas flowed every day as she walked and listened to the waves licking the shoreline. But as soon as she sat at the computer, coherent thought left and crazy imaginings like Wills filled her addled brain. She didn't believe she was snapping, but were people aware when their hold on reality started to slip?

᜞᙭ TWO ᜞᙭

April 1928

"*You boys look so handsome.*"

He loved the sound of his mother's voice. Today was Easter and they had gone to the tailor for new Sunday clothes. "*Don't go getting into mischief and get yourselves dirty. Mr. Wilson will bring the car around in fifteen minutes.*"

He and Freddy were standing in front of the mirror in his parent's parlor. He didn't have to rise on tiptoe anymore to see himself, but Freddy did. William leaned down to pick up his younger brother.

"*You'll be tall enough soon,*" the almost-eleven year old said in his maturing voice. "*I couldn't see myself this time last year and you're growing a lot faster than I did.*"

"*Do you think I'll ever be as tall as you, William?*"

"*Sure you will. When we're all grown up, we'll be the same size. Heck, you might even be taller.*"

"*I've got three years to catch up to you.*"

William had a tender look for his brother. "*You'll never catch up to me in age, Freddy, but you might catch up in height.*" He ruffled the cherubic curls as he set him down. "*Mind your manners and don't get dirty before we leave for church.*"

18

"I can't come home for the next few weeks, at least. I have so much to do and I'm behind on my deadline. A visit will have to wait."

Her mother was pulling the guilt card, even threatening to come to Castine if she didn't come home.

"No! That's not an option right now. I need time. After I finish what I'm doing, I'll come up for a weekend. But that's it. No more. I'm not ready to be there. I want to see you, but I won't stay more than a day or two."

Her poor, gentle mother would be heartbroken if she knew the truth. Maisy didn't have any inclination to explain the pain she was suffering, so her easiest alternative had been to not confront it in the first place. She would have to deal with what to tell them soon. And she would, just as soon as she faced this uninspired manuscript.

She finally forced herself to sit until the requisite number of words had been written each day. Her legs and shoulders ached, and she knew she was writing a string of boring words with no passion, but at least she had something now. Even she was bored as she read them before hitting the 'send' button to Jonnell. She couldn't muster enough emotion to care.

"Did you finish what you needed to do?"

"Wills?"

"In the flesh . . . well, figuratively, but yes, I'm here."

"Where have you been?"

"Right here. I haven't left. You made it clear you wanted solitude, and I didn't want to intrude while you seemed to be figuring out whatever it was that had you troubled."

"I've been writing my boring manuscript about a boring girl and her boring friend and their boring boyfriend. Not very exciting."

"You're done then?"

"Only with a teaser. My editor will call and tell me she doesn't like what I've done, then I'll try to figure out how to gain a little more time until some kind of inspiration hits me. I'll even try to care enough to do what she suggests."

"Why don't you find a different topic?"

"Why don't you stop prying in my affairs?"

"As you wish."

"Wait! Don't go! I'm sorry. I didn't mean to be testy. You've been nothing but gracious."

"I'm a figment of your imagination, so I don't have many alternatives."

"Are you?"

"Am I what?"

"A figment of my imagination?"

"I don't know. Am I?"

"I don't have a clue. You must be."

"Then it must be as you say."

"Don't leave."

"I'm not going anywhere."

"Promise?"

"Promise."

"I'm so tired. And weary. That was draining."

"Your boring story about the boring people and their boring relationship? What was draining about it?"

"I don't know. Having to write it. I knew when I was writing that I didn't want to think about the heartache of such a story, but I had to have a certain number of words to send Jonnell."

"Why didn't you want to think about it?"

"I just didn't." She hesitated. "It's not a subject I have an interest in pursuing."

"Then at the risk of repeating myself, why don't you write about something else?"

"Because this is the idea I pitched before the accident, and now I have no desire to write the story. But it's been too long, she's been considerate in giving me time, and now I have to give her results."

"How did you send the draft to her?"

"What do you mean?"

"I saw you at your fancy typewriter, but I never saw paper, and you never left to mail a package, so how did you send it?"

"By email, of course."

"Email?"

She frowned. "Where are you?"

"Right here."

"Right where?"

"Beside you."

Did she just want so much for him to be real? Obviously no one was in the room with her. Her walk would do her good today. What she'd sent Jonnell was trash and she knew it. She'd have to reimburse them for the advance if she couldn't come up with a plausible storyline. She needed a break and would make plans to go home that weekend. She had left not visiting her family for too long.

کردہ؟

"I'm glad to see you. I was worried you wouldn't come back," he said.

21

She set her suitcase down and one side of her mouth curled as she locked the door. "And I didn't think you'd still be here after I had time away."

"Where would I go?"

"How would I know? I don't even know where you are."

"Have you been crying?"

"Why would you think that?"

"Because it's something you do a lot."

"That's none of your business."

"How was your trip?"

She gave his question serious consideration. "It was good to see my parents."

"And?"

"And the rest of it doesn't matter. I'm old enough I can choose who I want to be with. I'd never go back if it weren't for my folks."

"Did you visit with friends?"

"I don't have friends anymore."

"Because that's the way you want it?"

Was that the way she wanted to live? "I suppose so. There aren't many people I trust enough to be friends with."

"Have you always been that way?"

"No, but it's the way I am now."

"Are you doing what you want to do?"

"Partly. Two goals in my life have been to be an author and to travel. I'm not in any condition to do one, but I'm working on the other."

"Where would you like to go?"

"What's with the twenty questions?"

"Trying to figure out who you are. I've watched you for almost two years now, and you're a strange mixture of strength and weakness."

"*What?*"

"You're a strange combination . . ."

"I heard that part. Two years?"

"That's how long you've been here."

"I'm aware of how long I've been here. How long have *you* been here?"

"It seems like forever, but I've inhabited these walls almost seventy-five years, I think."

She collapsed on the couch. "This is a joke, right?"

"It's not very funny if it is."

"Who are you, Wills?"

"Why don't you unpack? You've had a long day, long weekend. We'll talk in the morning."

"So you'll be here?"

"I promise you I'm not going anywhere."

"Until when?"

"That's one of the matters we can discuss. And may I mention how impressed I am with how simply you've decorated the cottage? I was more inclined to open windows and let in nature instead of cluttering my surroundings with possessions that would tie me down. You've done a superb job of making it cozy and neat."

"Thank you for noticing. My home brings me pleasure every day . . . even though you think all I do is cry."

She went to her bedroom and shut the door. Immediately she reopened it. "Can you see me in here?"

"If I wanted to I could. I'm too much of a gentleman to consider such an intrusion."

"Thank God for small favors."

"Excuse me?"

"Nothing."

She stood at the sink the next morning watching waves fling themselves against the rocky shoreline.

"Looks like we have a tempest blowing in."

She didn't move as she waited for her pulse to slow, closing her eyes and trying to understand what was happening.

"I loved being here when a squall reminded us of the power of nature," he said.

"Was this your home?"

"My father and I built this as a retreat."

"You built Summerset?"

The gentle rumble was soothing. "I've always liked that you called her that. I was never so imaginative and only referred to her as The Cottage."

She had purchased her sanctuary toward the end of summer two years ago and spent her first six months barely leaving, loving the wind and the rains battering her refuge, the walls somehow living for her when she didn't want to.

"There are a few housekeeping items to address before winter comes again. I'll tell you how."

"If you're real, why don't you take care of them yourself?"

Silence.

"Are you real?"

Still silence.

"That's what I thought." She turned back to her porcelain sink to finish the morning dishes and water the profusion of flowers gracing her windowsill. Reds, yellows, and purples, her plants brought her continual joy.

"I would if I had the ability. I'll explain what should be done when the time comes, but I'll need your hands to accomplish those tasks."

Her head bowed. She was totally confused.

"I don't want you to be frightened."

"I'm talking to a man who's lived in my house for seventy some-odd years. Why would I possibly be frightened?"

"You'll get used to the strangeness of the situation."

"Wait! Wills! William! Are you William Andrew Raines?"

"I am. I was."

"It's your grave south of the house?"

"It is."

"Is that why you can't leave?"

"That's a broad explanation for my quandary. But I have been thankful more times than I can count that someone had the foresight to bury me here and not at the home of my betrayer."

"Oh, Wills. What happened?"

He was silent long enough she feared he wouldn't answer.

"Can I ask you to meet me in the study?" he said, breaking the silence.

The laughter bubbled. "Of course I'll meet you in the study. That's perfectly normal, isn't it?"

Wiping her hands and folding the dishtowel was normal, hanging the towel on the rod was normal. Meeting a voice in the study? Sure, perfectly normal.

"Is this a personal conversation? Shall I shut the door?" She recognized her nervousness and wondered why she had actually come to the office.

"The door wouldn't stop me, but I think it's better for now if you leave it open."

"So I can run?"

"If you need to."

That gave her pause.

"I like that you're growing your hair out. It's more flattering than the short blonde hair you had when you arrived. The way it frames your face makes you appear softer, and the brown highlights bring out the cognac color in your eyes."

"Cognac. I like that. I've never thought of them that way before." She stepped to the mirror to look at her eyes and the awkward length of her hair.

"I keep thinking about cutting it because it's hard to manage." But she wouldn't. Josh had hated when she grew it long. She would continue to grow it out. "But thank you. I like it darker too."

She didn't collapse when she briefly saw someone's reflection standing next to her. She couldn't breathe with the speed of her pulse and the scream lodged in her throat. When she was able, she turned slowly to see who was there.

No one.

"What's the matter?"

"Nothing. Nothing at all."

"You seem upset."

"I was a little frightened. I thought I saw someone."

"Was it a man or a woman?"

"A man." Without moving, her eyes scanned the room, but she was alone.

Goosebumps rose on her arms, puzzled at what she'd seen. Straightening a few papers on her desk, she saw movement again and her eyes darted to the mirror.

"Please don't be afraid."

Would her chest explode if her heart beat this fast for long?

They stood silently, staring. Her eyes explored his

height, his rugged handsomeness, the blondish-brown hair that fell casually over his forehead, and flawless arched brows that framed the bluest eyes she'd ever seen. No part of her understood what was happening, and her heart was beating double time.

"You can see me, can't you, Maisy?"

Her eyes roamed the mirror, seeing him behind her, knowing if she turned he wouldn't be there.

Her voice was a whisper. "Yes."

His shoulders relaxed. "It's been over sixty years."

Her brow furrowed.

"No one's seen me in over sixty years."

"Where have you been?"

"I've been right here," he said, almost morosely.

She thought of all the people who must have been here, but of course she couldn't yet grasp what he was telling her.

"Not that this craziness makes sense, but if no one has seen you in six decades, why do you look like that?"

His expression was puzzled.

"Why do you look like a young man?"

"Oh, that. You're seeing me as I was in 1945. I haven't aged."

She sank to her chair. "Are you dead?"

He considered how best to answer her. "What do you think?"

"How in the world am I supposed to know what I think? I'm talking to you, aren't I?"

"Yes."

"But you're dead?"

"My body is no longer here."

"That makes perfect sense." She laid her head on her arm on the desk. "Is this *The Twilight Zone*?"

"Excuse me?"

"You know, Rod Serling? *The Twilight Zone?*"

His brow raised as his head tilted.

"*Traveling beyond another dimension. A land of shadow and substance. A wondrous journey unlocked by the key of imagination.* Are you telling me I've crossed into *The Twilight Zone?*"

"I'm afraid I don't understand."

"Of course you don't. How could you?"

She stared at his chiseled chin, the dimples that were barely evident as he stared back, and the combination of features that made him undeniably attractive.

"What's going through your brain?" His voice was soft.

The edges of her lips turned up. "Just trying to decide what level of crazy this rises to."

"I'd say your mental instability is well defined, but my existence in your life is not part of your imbalance." He winked as they exchanged a grin.

They continued to observe each other. When she turned toward the room, no one was there.

"Not everything can be understood with our restricted intelligence," he said sympathetically.

"But you're here?"

He nodded. "In this place and time, I'm real."

"Because you love being here?"

"No man loves his jail." After a moment he said, "The mirror allows you to see me."

"And you can see me?"

"Yes. But I don't need the mirror. I've watched you struggle and triumph. I've been captivated by your beauty and been lost in your eyes long before you brought the mirror home."

"Dear Lord." She felt his warm response. "Why are you here?"

"For similar goals as yours."

"What's that supposed to mean?"

"You're here because you're working through concerns you need to resolve, searching for peace, for release. I'm here for the same reasons."

She stood abruptly and turned, angry. "How do you presume to tell me why I'm here? This is my home. Where else would I be?"

"I'm not trying to ruffle your feathers, I'm merely making an observation."

"You're a ghost. Stop meddling in my affairs."

He ignored her comment. "There is a difference, however, in our presence here. I need your assistance to be able to escape the prison of these walls if I'm going to find peace."

"Mine? What can I possibly do for you?"

"All in due time, Maisy."

"Why did you pick that name to call me?" His familiarity was suddenly frustrating.

"Margaret is much too formal. The common nicknames don't suit you. Maisy is young and lighthearted and carefree – the characteristics that are natural to your essence, you've just lost sight of them for a while."

"I'm not going to stand here and be psychoanalyzed by someone who doesn't exist."

She grabbed a jacket with a hood. "Please don't go out in this weather," he said. "I'll be silent and not say another word."

She slammed the door as she stepped outside. *How dare he?* The wind whipped her skin and knife strokes of lightning slashed across the open skies as she hurried to the shoreline for a quick morning jog. She was foolish to be out in this but hoped some self-inflicted pain would lessen the memory of his words . . . and his breathtakingly fascinating face.

❧ THREE ❧

September 1929

"It's your first cotillion, Freddy. The girls will be shy, but they'll expect you to ask them to dance, so follow my lead. I'll show you the ropes."

"I'm almost as tall as you are," Freddy said as they stood side by side in front of their mother's mirror. "Either you're slowing down or I'm speeding up."

"Since I'm still growing, you must be growing faster. Keep it up, little brother."

They pushed each other good naturedly as William showed Freddy how to tie his tie. "You look handsome. All the girls will want a turn on the dance floor with you."

"Do you have your eye on anyone special?" Freddy asked.

"Yeah, there's only one girl for me. I'm going to marry her one day."

"I'm kinda sweet on someone too. Who's yours?"

He walked out the door with a dimpled smile. "Like I'd tell my big-mouthed little brother."

"*T*hank you for not being gone long."

She was wind-blown but dry. The rain hadn't started by the time she got home.

"Ah, you're still here." Rather than calming down, the pain in her leg had her itching for a fight.

"I told you, I'm confined within these walls."

"What makes you think for a minute I'm like *you*? That I'm not at peace? What else would I be but peaceful in this environment?"

He remained silent as she went to the kitchen, rummaging in the refrigerator to give her something to occupy herself, settling on a bottle of water, then slamming the door so he'd know she didn't appreciate his interference.

"Forgive me, but there haven't been many days since you arrived when I haven't watched you cry, haven't heard you talk in your sleep about people and places that aren't here."

"Don't you consider eavesdropping an invasion of privacy? This is *my* house! How dare you!"

"Again, my apologies. Unfortunately, our dwelling is a small space and I have nowhere to go to not hear you, to not feel your pain, to be helpless in not being able to extend you comfort."

"I don't need your comfort. I need to be left alone so I can finish my work." She picked up her keys and purposefully pulled the door to the garage hard enough behind her for the walls to rattle.

The skies were black and threatening. After driving in circles, she found herself in front of the well-manicured home of Sarah and Jonathan. Sarah must have seen her sitting there because she came out of the house with a welcoming wave and approached the late model, sensible grey sedan she had purchased after the accident. The accident . . . she didn't want to think about it.

"Well, good morning. What brings you out in this weather?" Sarah asked in a friendly manner, talking above the rising winds. She obviously had no concept of the turmoil that pushed Margaret out of her comfort zone to arrive at this point.

"Good morning." She didn't want to sound grudging. It's not as though Sarah had sought *her* out. "I was wondering," she tried to make her voice friendlier, "do you know about the families who lived in my house before?"

"*Jonathan?*" she called loudly, keeping her eyes focused on her visitor. "Would you come out here?"

Wiping his hands on a rag, a cheerful countenance on his face, the screen door banged in the wind as he approached them while she continued to sit uncomfortably in her car. "Margaret's asking if you can tell her about the people who used to live in her home?"

"Sure I can. Been in my family since it was built. Something in particular you want to know?" Their friendliness was inviting, but she didn't want to make friends, especially not ones who would be leaving soon.

"Wondering who owned it before I did?" She was shouting against the weather. "Sarah said the mirror I bought came from my house originally. How did it get to your house? Nothing specific, just general information."

"I made a fresh pot of coffee and Sarah just took some of the best cinnamon rolls out of the oven you will ever taste in the state of Maine. Come in out of this gale and I'll tell you what I know." Without waiting for a response, he was hurrying toward the house.

"Come on," Sarah said as she opened the car door from the outside. "Jonathan knows more than most about the area. He can answer your questions."

"I really shouldn't . . ." She hesitated. What was she doing?

"Yes, you should. We won't be around forever, and you should be acquainted with the history of your little place so you can pass the information on. That's how it's done around here, word of mouth."

They both ran to the house, hair tousled, wet by the time they got inside. There were neatly stacked boxes everywhere, but even in its disarray it was easy to tell the home was clean and well organized. Following her into the kitchen, Sarah took a stack of papers off a classic turquoise 1950's metal and vinyl chair and motioned for her to sit.

"We've been going through things, trying to figure out what's important and what's not. Years of accumulation. It doesn't look like it, but we're close to being done. Coffee?" she asked, pulling mismatched mugs from pine cupboards that appeared to be original to the house.

"Thank you." Maisy pushed the strands of hair out of her face and tried to pull it all back into the ponytail to get it out of her face.

"Cream and sugar?"

"No, just black."

Husband and wife worked amicably, setting out plates and napkins and silverware. Within minutes they were relaxing comfortably. "So where do you want me to start?" he asked.

"I'm not sure. How about starting at the beginning and tell me what you can?"

"That's easy enough."

Sarah poured a cup of coffee and nudged the steaming brew toward him as the shutters on the house rattled. With a nod of acknowledgement at his wife, he began what sounded like an often-repeated tale.

"Andrew Raines was a wealthy businessman in Kennebunkport. He and his wife, Eva, had two sons, William and Freddy. Andrew and William took on a spring and summer project in 1936 when the country was still in the throes of the Great Depression and built themselves a summer home.

"Well-to-do when so many were struggling, they could have whatever they wanted, but Andrew was a simple man at heart who enjoyed working with his hands. He adored his wife, and she longed for the simpler times in their lives, so he built them a two-bedroom cottage with help every now and then from local laborers who needed work. When the house was finished, Andrew brought your mirror to their cottage from the big house because it was one of Eva's prized possessions."

"Then how did you end up with it?" Maisy asked.

"I'll get to that part," he said, smiling. "William was killed in Africa during World War II and his father never recovered from his loss."

Sarah reached over and touched Maisy's arm when she saw the tears standing in her eyes. Maisy gave her a slight nod and moved her hands to her lap, trying to fit the puzzle pieces together.

"Go on, please," she said quietly.

"Freddy and his wife had two boys, Willie and James. They'd spend summers here when the boys were little. Freddy became an alcoholic and I hear he had quite a temper. The man Sarah and I bought this house from, Roger Schierholz, also had two sons.

"One day he took his boys over to see if Willie and James wanted to play. According to him, Freddy was wild-eyed when he answered the door, said his boys weren't home but insisted Roger take the mirror that very day. While he had admired it on occasion, Roger thought giving away such a personal but valuable possession was immensely strange.

"When we bought the property, Mr. Schierholz left the mirror with us since it had come from my family originally and he had often been uncomfortable in the peculiar way he acquired it. Sarah and I were talking the other day about how pleased we are it's found its rightful home and is back in the cottage where it belongs."

Maisy's mind was spinning at the stories she'd heard. "Who's lived there since?"

"The day he got rid of the mirror was the last day Freddy and his family ever visited. Eva came out a few times, but the house was vacant until Willie and James grew up. Ownership stayed in the family but the place sat empty except for an occasional visit. My brother Donovan bought it about a decade ago, but didn't like the humidity here, so he sold it. And you know the rest," he said pleasantly.

She was numb.

"Do you want more coffee?"

"No, thank you, Sarah. I have to head home."

"Why don't you wait it out until the rain's not so heavy?"

"I appreciate you taking the time to share the story with me, but I really have to go. It gives me a new appreciation for what I have."

"You come back any time. Door's always open," Sarah called to her as she raced for her car.

"I'm sorry." She hung her keys in their proper place in her orderly home and took her soaking wet jacket to the laundry room. When she received no response, she repeated it as she took off her waterlogged tennis shoes. Still being met with silence, she said, "Don't pout, it's unbecoming a gentleman."

"Were you speaking to me?"

"Who else would I be talking to? Of course I'm speaking to you." She took the rubber band from her hair and shook the wet strands out with her fingers.

"Then what exactly are you sorry for?" he asked.

"Trying to wrap my brain around this . . . you . . . here . . . for years . . . without thinking I'm loony, that I've lost my marbles, that you're not a figment of my imagination."

"It's hard to accept the non-tangible realms when you're tied to a body."

"Do you find it strange – visible but invisible? Here but not really?"

"I've had decades to ponder the idea. At first I was overcome with the loss of my shadow. Now my transparency seems perfectly normal."

"Normal. I'm not sure I remember what that is."

"I assure you, you're not crazy. Well, at least not in regards to me."

Tilting her head, she said, "So we have to live together as long as I'm here? That will be awkward."

"Trust me, I'll be gone as soon as I'm able, but I can't move on without your help."

"So you've said. I hope my presence hasn't given you desires beyond my ability to take care of them."

"I know you, Maisy. I know what you're capable of and I know your heart."

"What exactly do you need from me?"

"Have you got a few minutes?"

"Do I appear to be busy?"

"Let's sit in the study then. I'm rather fond of conversing with you face to face."

Her bare feet were cold as she settled at her desk, so she tucked them beneath her. She saw him standing next to her in the mirror and took a deep breath to calm her pulses. Trapped in the hard grip of his scrutiny and the manly combination of his features, she said, "You're disturbingly handsome." Her voice caught at her random comment. "You must have been quite the ladies' man when you were alive."

"Your blush is captivating," he said, "but if you have a desire to say what's on your mind, don't be embarrassed by the words you express."

"Are you ignoring my question?" Her cheeks were still stained with heat.

"It wasn't really a question." One side of his delightful lips turned upward, then he looked to a place beyond her. "I was pursued, I will admit, but I only had eyes for one woman during my lifetime."

"What was her name?"

"Mary Catherine." His expression darkened. Margaret was intrigued.

"What happened?"

"That's what I need you for." He paused, then captured her with his intensely blue gaze. "I want you to write a book. My spirit won't rest until my story has been told. Only then can I be set free from the chains that bind me to this ethereal existence."

"What? What good can I be to you? I can't find words to express anything anymore."

"I've watched you. I've listened to you. You've lacked passion for your subject matter, but not for your writing. You're trying to write about situations you haven't wanted to pursue. I believe if you and I get to be friends, you'll want to tell my story."

"Did you just call me boring?"

A stunning smile crossed his face. "If the shoe fits . . ."

She gasped and turned to teasingly slap him, but there was no one there. Her laugh hung in the air.

"You'll get used to this new dimension, I promise. I'm glad the mirror is here so we can communicate face to face. You won't feel quite so unbalanced."

"Don't presume to know what I feel since even I don't have a clue."

"My apologies. I'll keep that in mind."

"Wills?"

"Yes?"

"Did she love you as much?"

"I thought she did."

Her sob burst from seemingly nowhere.

"Are you crying for me or for you?"

"Yes," she said pitifully.

"Are you aware you cry often?"

She stood and walked to the door. "Are you aware you're interfering?"

"Forgive me, but I have the advantage of having been acquainted with you for a long time. You're just getting to know me, so let's give the arrangement a little time."

"Getting to know you . . . I'm not getting to know you. I'm talking to a voice in an empty room that's always felt harmless. Now I'm off balance and not sure where there might be a safe haven."

"You will never have anything to fear from me, you have my word. I'll never speak again if my presence gives you concern. You can go back to thinking you imagined me."

Her throaty response emerged from deep within. "Imagined you? Now that I've heard your voice and seen your face, there will be no going back. Looks like we're stuck with each other."

"Only for a while. When we come to the end of the path set before us, I will leave you in peace. I promise."

Her eyes rose to gauge his sincerity, her breath stopping at the reflection of his golden grin that rivaled the glow of the setting sun on the horizon.

"When the time comes, I'm not sure that's a promise I'll want you to keep."

❧ FOUR ❧

June 1936

"It must be nice to be the favorite child."

"What are you talking about? Have you been drinking, Freddy?"

"Yeah, whadaya gonna do about it, big brother?"

"Where did you get the alcohol?"

"I opened the dining room cabinet. Voila."

"How much have you had?"

"Obviously not enough."

"Tell me what's wrong."

"It's always about you. 'William graduated top in his class.' 'William will take over the family business.' 'William will help me build the cottage in Castine.' You look so much like him it's sickening - like you were spit out of his mouth."

"All you have to do is step in at any time. There's no favoritism. You just never show an interest. I'd love for you to be involved."

"I don't want anything to do with your crappy cottage. Can you imagine me doing something so plebian as to carry lumber and drive a nail? Heaven help me. But even if I was there, you'd still be the crowned prince."

"Now you're being fanciful."

"Fanciful like asking Mary Catherine out and finding she only has eyes for you?"

Pain shot through William's chest at the words. "You asked Mary Catherine out?"

"What? You think you have a market on all the pretty girls? I've been smitten with her since we were kids. I had no idea she was your flame. But it figures, doesn't it? William gets whatever William wants."

"What's gotten into you? That's not fair and you know it."

Freddy threw his whiskey at William. William ducked in time, but the leaded glass snifter hit the bottom right corner of their mother's prized mirror.

"Good God, Freddy. Now look what you've done."

"Tough," he said. He grabbed his jacket. "You're the one who can sweet talk his way out of any situation. You tell her what happened. Then it will all be okay because it's coming from you." He slammed the door behind him.

⁊ℭ∤ℛℬ

"**Y**es, I understand, Jonnell. Of course I understand the position I've put you in. Can I just tell you . . . No, I get it, but let me run something by you . . . Sure. Bye."

Maisy looked at the rug absently to see if she was making it threadbare where she paced when she was talking on the phone or thinking through ideas.

"You seem upset." His voice was close.

"There are too many nuances of this story I don't want to explore."

"Would you show me how you were talking to her?"

"What do you mean?"

"How do you communicate with her? It's like a walkie-talkie, but she's a hundred miles away."

"Of course you wouldn't know about cell phones." She picked hers up to try to explain. "There are towers and satellites that transmit information and beam radio waves to devices. And you're right. Cell phones are like a walkie-talkie, only much more sophisticated. There are more electronics in this gadget than there were on the spaceship that landed a man on the moon."

He laughed. "For a minute I thought you were serious."

"About what?"

"A man on the moon."

"I was serious. That happened long before I was born."

"Truly? How far the world has come in such a short time."

"Do you know what a television is?"

"I've heard it mentioned a few times, but I've never seen what I assume is a box that shows motion pictures."

"And my computer, have you looked at it?"

"Is that the fancy machine you type on? But there is never paper in it. I've observed you staring at the light for hours, but I didn't want to invade your privacy, so I wasn't sure what you were doing."

"Watching movies, watching TV – or television, reading books, writing letters, writing books, buying things. And you're right, just staring . . . people can waste their lives on this little machine."

"I've often wondered why you don't have friends over."

Her focus shifted. "That's different. I don't have anyone over because I don't *want* anyone over. I want to be alone."

"Like Greta Garbo?"

Amusement struck her. "Your wit is quick, I'll give you that."

"Your desire to be alone makes our living arrangement rather inconvenient, doesn't it?" he asked.

"I'll adjust to having you here."

"I have one more question."

"I'll try to answer it."

"Who is Siri?"

Her smile was immediate. "How do I explain that she is a voice who lives in my phone? But not just a voice, she's a computer who understands my commands. When I say, 'Hey, Siri,' she knows it's a command to listen up. I'll show you sometime."

"It doesn't appear to be complicated, but with no knowledge of the advancement of technology in dozens of years, it's impressive."

"Even for me it's impressive. Discoveries have progressed so much in the last decade it's hard to keep up. Now go occupy yourself. I have work to do."

"As you wish."

She checked her email, poured over revisions Jonnell sent, all the while conscious she wasn't alone.

"This is going to be harder than I thought," she said.

"What do you mean?"

"Knowing you're here. Being conscious of your presence, feeling you without being able to touch you."

"I should probably be sorry. I'm not. You have no idea how long I've wanted to talk with someone."

She looked up to the glass that returned his reflection. There was a certain grace about him and she felt no threat.

His grin was mischievous. "And if I may be so bold, it doesn't hurt that you're cute as a bug's ear."

"That's an old-fashioned expression." She blushed at his compliment.

"It's all I know." He shrugged, but his smile was tender.

"What do you need from me, Wills?"

"What did your agent say?"

"That she wants me to change most of what I wrote. That she wants me to add passion to the pages. That she wants to feel some emotion and not just figure out how long it will take to trudge through it."

"Can you present her with another story? Tell her you'll finish this one after she let's you write a different kind of novel first?"

"What do you have in mind?"

"I need someone to chronicle my journey, Maisy. I need to let the proper people know so I can be released from this prison of long dark nights that inevitably end in short chilly days."

"What shall I tell Jonnell?"

"Tell her you have a dramatic adventure of a ghost who will not rest until the tragedy of his brother's ultimate betrayal is told, a narrative of love and war and murder. And if she reads your new tale and has no interest, at the very least my misfortune will be recorded and my spirit will be set free for its next voyage, its next level of consciousness."

"Jonnell says I have two months to suspend my other writing if I think I can make a go of this book. Historicals are popular right now, but I'll have to give her my work in progress every week so she trusts I'm really working on something worthwhile."

"What do *you* want, Maisy?"

"What I've wanted since I started getting better is to be a *New York Times* bestselling author. I've written a couple of books that were fairly successful, but they weren't record breaking the way they were expected to be."

"We should be able to produce a readable book out of this saga of intrigue."

"I hope so. She's going to hold my feet to the fire and keep tight reins on me so she knows I'm not still blowing smoke."

"Blowing smoke?"

"Never mind." That was an expression she didn't care to explain.

"What did you do before you came here?"

"I taught middle school English. Traci worked at a local school when we graduated college, and she got me a job."

"Who's Traci?"

She focused on the budding leaves that multiplied and changed daily out her window. "She was my best friend."

"Was?"

"Was."

"What happened?"

Her eyes were on her surroundings, avoiding her life before. "We don't speak."

"You talk about her a lot."

She turned abruptly. "What do you mean?"

"You call out her name in your sleep. I've wanted to ask you who she is in your life."

"No one. She's no one in my life."

"Did you see her when you visited your parents recently?"

"She came over."

"And?"

She was pacing, holding her elbows, running from her thoughts.

"And nothing. I didn't want to see her so I didn't engage. That's it."

She wasn't ready to talk about Traci and he didn't want to agitate her. "How did you end up buying a cottage in Castine?"

The shimmering water in the distance grounded her. "I was in the hospital for a few months after the accident. One of the nurses kept talking about this little town in Maine where her family spent summers. I love the shore and she made being here sound peaceful, so I did research and found Summerset was for sale. I had insurance money coming and I hated Winslow and didn't want to be there, and I didn't want to move to Augusta to be near my folks, so I bought it."

She stood at the door of her office and observed him in the mirror. His face was achingly captivating, his voice and demeanor gentle. "Can you tell me about the accident?"

Her focus shifted to a time she wanted to forget. "Not much to tell. It was raining and we went off the road. Josh was thrown from the car and died, I was trapped. I was conscious long enough to dial nine-one-one. Next thing I remember, it was a week later and I was waking up in traction in the hospital."

"What's nine-one-one?"

She would have to be more considerate when she spoke to him.

"On my phone, I can press the buttons – nine-one-one – and it connects me on the other end to an emergency operator. They find where you are and send either the police or fire department or an ambulance, whatever it is you need."

"That's a remarkable service."

"Another noteworthy feature, as in my case, I couldn't tell them where I was, but they were able to electronically locate my phone to find me. In the dark and the rain, no one would have found us at least until the next day."

"How long after the accident did you come here?"

"Let's see. The accident was in early March and I moved here toward the end of August. I had to learn to walk again before they'd release me."

"You've come a long way since you arrived. I've been proud of your tenacity."

"My mother had a fit because she wasn't going to be here to take care of me, but I assured her daily walks along the bluff would strengthen my leg."

"You have no idea how painful it was for me to watch you fall and not be able to help you."

"Oh, God, you saw me? Lying on the floor, bawling like a baby?"

"It was hard to miss."

Their shared amusement was musical.

"I didn't think I'd survive that first winter. I stocked up on food because I expected to be snowbound, but the season wasn't nearly as bad as I anticipated."

"The garage was a stroke of genius."

"Thanks," she said, proud she'd had the addition built. "There were a few days when the snow was deep enough, I knew I didn't have the stamina to get to my car much less clear at least a hundred pounds of the white stuff off in case of an emergency, so building the garage was the first order of business I took care of when the weather permitted."

"I wanted so much to help you, but you kept going,

even when putting one foot in front of the other was obviously not your inclination."

She remembered those early months. "I sometimes fantasized that they'd find my body here during the spring thaw."

"I had such respect for you. You were delicate but tenacious. Even in your abject sorrow and what was clearly a lot of pain, you did what needed to be done to survive."

"I didn't want to."

"Survive?"

"Mm hmmm."

"You're a prime example of the will to survive. It's amazing how much you want to live when death threatens."

She searched his face. "Is that how it was for you?"

"You mean did I want to survive?"

"It sounds silly when you put it that way." She blushed.

"Yes, Maisy, I wanted to survive. I couldn't believe I was going to die. I'd survived hell, then suddenly met my demise."

"What happened?"

"You'll hear the story and help right the wrongs of my death. All in good time." He appeared to be standing near enough to touch her. "Do you miss him?"

A lifetime went through her mind as she considered how to best answer his question. "No," she said, walking from the room.

FIVE

July 1937

"I'm so proud of what a man you were in helping your father."

"Thank you, Mother. Working with my hands alongside him was a keen way to spend the summer, and we ended up with a swell place."

Her radiance lit her face. "I love everything about being here."

"You must if you brought your treasured mirror all the way from home."

"But just think, William. You can stare at the reflection and see the wind blowing in the trees, get lost on the waves. Nature's majesty is duplicated right here and we don't even have to leave the comfort of the room." She stood with her arm around his waist and helped him see life from her positive perspective.

"But now it's time for you to feed your starving family. You won't have your normal staff to cook for you when we're here."

"Having to work is one of the bonuses. It reminds me of simpler times when your father and I were first married and he labored with his hands."

"You can't tell me you mind all the benefits that come with

his wealth?"

"Of course not. But being the couple who is in love will be easier when the world isn't pulling him in different directions."

"I understand that. We'll have decades of memories here."

*T*hey were having a quiet discussion late the following afternoon when they heard footsteps on the porch before the brass lion head knocker tapped on the front door. Maisy and Wills exchanged a silent glance as she got up to answer the interruption. No one ever came to her house.

"Hi, Sarah, what can I do for you?" Maisy didn't want to be discourteous and not invite her in, but she was afraid of what Sarah might be able to see. Would the mirror show her the same reflections Maisy enjoyed?

Sarah peeked beyond the open door trying to glimpse the tidy cottage that none of the locals had ever been inside. Maisy stepped onto the porch and pulled the door closed behind her.

"Jonathan and I finished sorting our belongings a lot earlier than we expected so we're packed and ready to head out at the end of this week. Wanted to give you our number in Bangor in case you should need us." She handed Maisy a piece of paper.

"Thanks. I appreciate you thinking of me."

"House is boarded up. Jonathan's nephew is traveling now but will be here sometime next spring so you'll probably meet him then, and I'm sure we'll be back to visit often enough. We'll only be an hour away."

"Be sure to let me know when you're in town."

"We definitely will. Didn't expect to be leaving so

soon, but it's time. You have everything you need?" Sarah asked.

"Yes, I'm quite content, thank you."

"You're such a little slip of a thing. You take care of yourself. There are a lot of nice people here who would help you in a heartbeat. All you have to do is ask."

"I'll remember that. Good luck." A chilling breeze was blowing and Maisy felt guilty for her seeming lack of hospitality, so she gave her a hug instead to help lessen what might be perceived as rudeness.

She waved as Sarah got to her truck. "Thanks so much for my mirror!" She went inside and leaned against the door.

"It was fortuitous they were getting rid of the mirror." His voice was beside her.

Maisy peeked out the window to make sure they were alone. "Fortuitous indeed. But I was concerned she might be able to see you or hear you. I didn't want to be impolite, but I certainly wasn't going to let her come in."

"No one can see me if I don't want them to. Don't ever worry about that happening."

"Seriously? Then why didn't you communicate with me before?"

"There were innumerable times I wanted to. Being silent was difficult, and I had no ability to give comfort. You were so small and fragile."

"There's nothing fragile about me."

"I know that now. I almost collapsed when I saw you bring the mirror home. I knew my reality would be easier to prove if you were able to see me. Until then, there was no way to assure you that you weren't crazy, so silence seemed the better part of valor."

"That makes sense."

"Besides, you weren't ready then."

"How do you know?"

"I just do," he said kindly.

"Were you able to speak to me before the mirror returned?"

"Yes, at any time, but you can only see me because of the mirror. What I wanted most was to ease your sorrow but had no way to do that without scaring the bejesus out of you."

"Except for your initial contact, I wasn't frightened, just questioned my flight of fancy."

"Ah, yes, I was glad you had protection. Little good your bullets would have done against me, however," he said, examining his transparent arms.

She smiled at the memory. "When I bought the gun to stop a possible intruder, this wasn't exactly what I had in mind."

"Do you know how to use it?"

"My father was adamant that I be able to protect myself before he'd let me be here alone. I got rather proficient."

"Wise man. Even in a remote town like this, anything might happen. Heck, you never know who might show up unannounced."

"Very funny. What happened to you? Why are you still . . . hanging around?"

His immediate mirth amused her. "That's an apt description – hanging around. But don't you think 'floating around' might be more appropriate?"

"Wills, what can I do to help you?"

"I'm not the author, Maisy, and even if I were I'd have no way to convey what needs to be told. You're good at what you do."

"You can't possibly know that."

"I've watched you for a long time. I've heard you talking on the phone about how you think you're worthless as a writer, but when you're pacing and thinking through your stories, you're brilliant. I wish you knew how much."

"Dear Lord, you were listening?"

"Hard not to. Forgive me."

She pushed the hair out of her face. "I can conceptualize the book, but I can't seem to put the words on paper. My mind goes blank when I try to express what I'm feeling."

"Maybe if you have a distinctly different tale to tell it will motivate you. I have a saga that needs to be told, and you can embellish with whatever spin you want on the narration as long as the basic facts remain true. You're the one with the fascinating imagination."

"It's taken me all this time and I couldn't infuse passion into a story I had worked on for what seems like forever."

"I tried to understand what was holding you back. You ran away from getting involved and I had no idea why. I grieved that I couldn't grant you encouragement."

"Maybe one of these days I'll sit down with a bottle of wine and tell you how I came to be in Castine."

"I've never seen you drink."

"I haven't had a glass since the night of the accident."

She relaxed, knowing he was next to her.

"Is that what caused the accident?"

"No. Alcohol wasn't the reason, at least not for me and I was the one driving."

"We have all the time in the world, trust me. It will do you good to share your struggle when you're ready, but not until then. I'm a patient man."

"Obviously. Were you this understanding when you were alive?"

"My personality hasn't changed, if that's what you're asking."

"Mine has," she said bitterly.

"How so?"

"Believe it or not I used to be friendly and outgoing. Being popular was enjoyable."

He considered her words. "Do you miss the interaction?"

"Not at all." She didn't hesitate in answering. "That may appear selfish given your current circumstances, but being with others brings you pain. I'd rather be alone and interact with make-believe people I've dreamed up. They can't hurt you. Is that what you are, Wills?"

"Make believe? No, I assure you I'm real. A different type of real than what you've known, but real enough. But listen to me, Maisy, being hurt is part of life. You can't stop living because someone wounded you."

"What do you know about it?"

His laugh was swift and harsh. "You seriously ask *me* that question? There is evil around many of life's bends. I didn't arrive here by accident. I could have become bitter over the decades, but all I want is my freedom and to right the wrong done to me."

"I'm sorry. That was insensitive of me."

"Let's make a plan. We'll spend time together each day and I'll share my story. You'll be able to ask questions about details you might not understand because I want to make sure everything is clear. Then and only then will I be released to leave you in peace."

"We're not in a hurry, are we?" She wasn't anxious for

him to be out of her life, even if his existence was questionable.

"No. I want to show you elements of Summerset that will help you better deal with next winter. There are camouflaged areas concealing nothing of real value, just mementos of a bygone era. My dad was a trickster and he designed hiding places for the mental challenge."

"I'd swear I know this place like the back of my hand. I've spent a lifetime inside these walls in the past two years and I can't imagine any nook or cranny I'm not aware of."

"Life is full of surprises, is it not?"

"If I'm going to be crazy, it will be fun to be off balance with you."

"I would concur you're crazy, but I'm not part of your insanity, my Maisy."

Her tinkling laughter was like a ray of sunshine as he basked in her warm pool of light. "We've had enough time for you to trust in my existence – at least as much as is possible to believe with a finite human mind."

"Or to understand I'm completely batty and there's no hope for my feeble brain."

"Please tell me you're jesting."

"Of course I am. I'm as sane as I've felt in years, so don't wake me if I'm not."

"My wish is to show you how resilient you are before our journey is complete. I have such esteem for you, Maisy, and while you've hidden yourself out here away from civilization, you have so much to offer."

She walked away. "What can you possibly know about what I've secluded myself from?"

"I know you trust no one. That you're afraid to open up and let anyone in. That you write so you can be alone. That makes you as much a prisoner as I am."

"Or because this is the way I want to live."

"Right now you're broken and scarred, and I don't mean just physically, but mentally and emotionally as well. You're afraid to love, to allow someone close enough to hurt you."

"It's not like I can grow another heart."

"You've made yourself boring to try to prove you don't have one."

She started to respond, then laughter took over.

"What's so funny?" he asked.

"I'm sitting in the middle of nowhere with a man who's been dead for over seventy years, and his apparition is telling me I'm boring. Can there be a more ringing endorsement than that?"

Her perception of the conversation had him joining in her joyfulness.

"Ah, Maisy, you are a bountiful treasure. I pray someday you find someone who will truly appreciate your brains and savvy sense of humor."

She stopped laughing. "I'm content to be exactly where I am. I'm in no hurry to break the chains that bind us here, to this place, to this time, to each other. Let's enjoy the journey while we have this season of life together, Wills. If and when the time comes that this ends, I don't want regrets."

"When the time comes, we will both be enriched from having known the other," he said affectionately.

"Have you changed your walking route?" he asked as she hung her sweater on the hook.

"No, why?"

"Because you're doing so much better. When you first arrived your walk would take at least an hour. Now you're down to forty minutes. I wanted to congratulate you."

"Why are you timing me?"

"Quite frankly, at first when you'd leave the house I would panic thinking you might not return. I set my watch to time how long you were gone, and then I understood there was some schedule to what you were doing."

"You have a watch?"

"No, silly. Just a figure of speech."

Her smiling eyes reminded him of the hue of Spanish sherry.

"As much as I craved being alone, I can't imagine not having the option," she said.

"When I first arrived, time slowed to a nauseating crawl. I feared my hell would be eternal isolation. Then when Freddy and my family would visit and I wasn't able to interact, and no one knew I was here, I wondered what I had done to deserve such punishment."

"Oh, Wills, how tragic. I'm so sorry."

"Don't be sorry. Just help me escape this prison of limbo that has me trapped behind bars of emotion with no avenue of tangible interaction."

Her chest churned as she watched the reflected expressions dance across his face.

"Speech was so much more eloquent in your day. Now we're a generation of one hundred and forty characters." Shaking her head, she said, "Don't ask. Was Freddy your brother?"

"Yes. I was three years older, but we were as different as night and day."

"Were you close?"

"All of our lives – until the end."

She waited for him to continue. When he didn't, she said, "I'll do everything I can to help you gain your freedom."

"And in the adventure, you will achieve your *New York Times* Bestseller status. What will you do with that?"

She grinned. "Nora Roberts said being a famous author ensures you will have the best seat in the restaurant and be left alone to enjoy your meal."

"That sounds like a worthwhile goal," he teased. "But either way, your achievements will be a win for both of us."

His words of encouragement didn't produce the excitement in her they should have.

SIX

November 1941

"We are two good-looking dandies, are we not?" William turned to straighten Freddy's cap. "Who would have thought we'd look this good in uniform?"

"We'd look good in whatever we decided to wear," Freddy said, flexing his muscles in front of the mirror that had charted their growth for years.

He took on a solemn expression. "I can be an ass at times, but I do love you. No matter what happens and no matter where we go or where we're stationed, I'd give my life to protect you."

William swallowed the lump in his throat and studied his brother's reflection. "You have only to ask and whatever is mine is yours." A smile split his pensive countenance. "Well, anything except Mary Catherine."

He didn't notice Freddy's expression as he turned from the mirror.

"But I need to ask a favor of you," William said. "For as long as possible, I'd like you to keep an eye on Mary Catherine for me. We eloped."

"You married her?" Freddy's voice was raised as he reacted to his brother. "I didn't think your relationship was that serious!"

"We've kept our wedding secret because of dad's illness and the War and the confusion. We didn't want to add to anyone's burden."

"I can't believe you married her!" Freddy was pacing and agitated.

"Is there a problem with that?"

"No, of course not. I just thought . . . I thought . . . never mind."

"What's going on?"

"Nothing. I promise, William, I'll manage things as long as I'm here. You have my word." He stuffed his cap in his pocket and ran fingers through his tousled hair.

"I know you will. I trust you with my life."

"I haven't heard any rumblings that we may be shipped out."

"Do what you can. Mary Catherine will be fine as long as I know you're watching out for her. Depending on how long we're in Algeria, I'm praying we'll be done and back soon."

"Ambitious of you. Let's hope that's the way your mission turns out. You're an officer, though. No telling where they'll send you after we defeat the Germans in North Africa."

"I'll write mom and tell her we're married when dad's feeling better. She'll be in good hands with you, Freddy. Watch out for them."

"I'll do everything I can to make their lives easier."

61

"*T*ell me about your brother."

"I spent a lifetime loving and protecting him, then found he was a rubber man with no backbone to hold him erect."

"Damning praise, indeed."

"It took decades for me to learn you can't blame the snake for its cold heart. Freddy was who he was. He was just holding true to his nature."

"And Mary Catherine?"

An elusive and undefined expression crossed his face. "They would visit here and I felt betrayed because she ended up loving my brother." Maisy gasped. "They had a son together. It took me years to get past my anger and sorrow to forgive her."

"Dear Lord. What changed your mind?"

"She only knew what he told her. She was a product of her time and had no control over the situation. She did her best with the cards she was dealt. In that regard, I suppose I can admire her, but I had to find some reason or I would have gone mad."

"You're a better man than I am."

"What do you mean?"

"I'm not sure I'll ever be able to forgive my betrayer."

"For your sake . . . for your health, I hope there comes a time when you *can* learn to accept their shortcomings. A wise man once said, 'Holding on to anger is like grasping a hot coal with the intent of throwing it at someone else. You are the one who gets burned.'"

"Wait a minute. You said they had a son together. Jonathan said they had two sons."

Pain wrenched his virile face. "Their older son was

mine."

"*What?*" She hadn't meant to yell, but she threw down her pen.

"That's part of what I need to tell you, part of their treachery."

"It's time for my walk," she said, trying to regain her composure. "I don't believe I've got the capacity to ever find that level of absolution, but I'll consider your words."

Their days became peaceful and intimate interludes of him sharing his often-painful memories, and her transcribing them into a riveting storyline. At the end of each week she sent chapters to Jonnell who often pronounced them brilliant and had very few recommended edits.

"What's gotten into you?" Jonnell asked one afternoon.

"I beg your pardon?"

"Your passion is back. The Margaret whose writing I fell in love with is back with a vengeance. I wait anxiously each Friday morning for your email, excited to read the next installment."

"Thanks, Jonnell. That means a lot to me."

"Well this one should pull us out of the hole and set us on a new track. The ghost aspect is brilliant."

Her smirk wasn't evident in her voice. "I thought the concept was a fun twist."

"Keep up the good work. And write faster. I can't wait to read the rest."

"Thank you, my friend. Thanks for believing in me and for giving me time to find my sea legs. I'll be forever indebted."

"You're going to make us lots of money, girly. It's not completely altruistic."

"Bye, Jonnell. I may or may not send you more."

She was laughing as she hung up.

"So she's pleased?" His endearing face caressed her soul. "What made you think you couldn't write?"

She pushed the chair back as she stood to pace. "When you're told often enough how boring you are, you tend to absorb the concept as truth." She was embarrassed she had said so much, thinking maybe Wills might believe Josh's words if he thought about them.

"He was a fool."

Her eyes darted to his. "He obviously believed what he was saying, he reminded me almost every day. He thought he was pushing me to excel, to do better. In retrospect, his major accomplishment was to sabotage my confidence."

"He didn't deserve you, Maisy. Don't continue to try to find truth in his lie. You are proving there was not a shred of fact in his hurtful allegations."

He reached to stroke her shoulder then turned over his transparent hand. "It has long grieved me that you will never know the comfort of my touch."

His words were soothing music to her heart. "Thank you," she whispered.

"No thanks needed. You're a remarkable woman whom I admire immensely. Now go take your walk before I become maudlin on you."

She carried in an armful of wood when she returned.

"Are we having a fire?"

"I love sitting beside the open flames. The breeze off the Bay was chilly so I thought I'd warm us up. Then one of us is going to have a glass of wine and the other is going to tell more of his story."

She crossed to her desk to get matches and saw him

next to her.

"I suppose it's time to reveal another treasure to the cottage." His grin was infectious, his smoldering eyes made her heart do strange flips.

"I'm all ears."

"Bring your matches to the living room, please."

The hearth was made from river rock and stretched the length of the room. "There were many times I thought surely you would find this and I wanted desperately to tell you when I saw you hauling wood, but you weren't ready for me to make my presence known, and my greatest fear was that you would leave and not come back. Your loss was something I wasn't prepared for."

"What was I supposed to have found?"

"My father loved to hide things in plain sight, and my mother wanted uncluttered space. The bench you sit on in front of the fire? Lift it."

"Lift it? It's rock. I can't possibly."

"Try, please."

Maisy grasped the lip of the hearth and pulled up. She was shocked not only at how easily the lid rose, but at the several years worth of cut firewood stored inside.

"Oh, my goodness!"

"My father and I chopped all of those logs the second summer we spent here. He engineered the cover to be lightweight enough so my mother would be able to lift it unaided, but concealed its presence enough that no one else would see it. Clever, yes?"

"Yes! I'm so excited! This is like Christmas. I hate chopping wood, hate even more having to carry in the twigs and logs. Plus, the job is heavy and messy. Thank you! I want to hug you!"

"And I as well, but your appreciation is all the thanks I

need."

"I wish I had known about this before."

"I wish you had too. I tried to tell you."

"What do you mean?"

"Over the years of being alone in this place, I worked at trying to figure out what I was and wasn't capable of. Do you remember those times you stood in that very spot, mulling over what you wanted to do?"

Her head tilted toward the direction of his voice. "Yes. What does that mean?"

"I had developed a different sort of mental telepathy. For instance, when you decided to hang the mirror on the north wall and I knew you'd be happier with it on the east, I made a suggestion."

"I remember changing my mind, but I never heard you say anything."

"No. I refined a way of speaking to you without using words. Sometimes you heard me, sometimes you didn't."

"For instance?"

"For instance, I believe you've always had . . . what shall we call it . . . a black thumb?"

Her lilting laughter filled him with delight. "That's a nice way of phrasing it."

"So I helped you discover what to do to make your plants grow. You must admit you have an impressive collection of flowers."

"Oh, my word! I was so proud of myself, but my success was yours all along."

"No, Maisy, the victory wasn't mine. You were learning how to do what needed to be done. The accomplishment was solely yours."

"I planted my plum tree the first spring I was here. I thought for sure I would enjoy the fruits of my labor, but I had one straggling plum that survived the birds and the elements, and now look at it. It's thriving."

"Ah, yes, your plum tree." His amusement was evident in his voice. "I watched you tend to it that first year and thought the poor little tree too stubborn to be conquered by human neglect."

Delight bubbled from her. "How unkind!" But she continued to giggle.

His voice mellowed. "I saw similarities between you and your wilted tree. You both needed time and nourishment to flourish."

She contemplated his words then nodded, not wanting to face the truth of what he said. "Okay, what else?"

"You weren't very, um, proficient, shall we say, at starting a fire."

"That's for darned sure. Never could figure out what I was doing wrong and, even when I could get a fire started, I didn't know why it fizzled out right away."

"Each time before you'd go out to collect firewood I would try to guide you to pick up *dead and dry* logs and not the green limbs you were so fond of bringing home."

"That is so funny! Is *that* what it was? Anything else?"

"The main one was whenever you would bring in firewood, my chivalrous soul found watching you deplorable because you had to do the work without help. When you were stacking firewood, I would try to get you to hear the word 'lift.'"

"Seriously? I heard the word over and over like a song you can't get out of your head, and wondered what I was supposed to be lifting. The seat was made of stone and the thought never occurred to me I would actually be able to raise it. Thank you for trying to watch out for me."

"Seeing you struggle wrenched my soul, but I knew if

you had to do it yourself it would be best for what you needed. You found your physical and emotional muscle, and each season brought you further than you had been. You never gave up."

"Don't paint what was happening with a rosy whitewash. I gave up every day."

"No you didn't, Maisy. You're a survivor! You were knocked down more times than I can remember, but got right back up. Every time you tried again. You cried and railed at your fate, then showed 'em who's boss. You roll with the punches beautifully. You're my hero."

The metal lantern on the front porch swayed to the wind's mad fancy, howling as fingers of cold air infiltrated small openings around windows. She wanted to see him. Wanted to touch him. Wanted him to share those words while she was wrapped in his arms.

"I feel all those emotions too. You're not alone in your frustration." The words came from in front of her.

"What emotions?" she asked.

"Wanting you to see me, to be able to touch me, to tell you what's in my heart."

Tears suddenly stood on her lashes. "How did you do that?"

"I've had years to work on the nuances of this form, much like you learning there are other dimensions than what you've previously known."

"Sometimes I want so much just for you to hold me."

"I touch you often, until I am rudely reminded of my restrictions."

"It's best we not go there, Wills. Unless you're going to help me light the fire, get out of my way." She sought to be cheery, but her voice caught, holding back her anguish.

"As a matter of fact, I *am* going to help you. Come see

what else is stored in the wood bin."

She lifted the lid and saw only wood. "At the other end are dozens of small paper bags. Freddy and I filled them with pinecones and twigs and pine needles, then mother melted candle wax into each and rolled them into tight tubes. They make excellent fire starters."

"Again it's like Christmas and a birthday combined. Think they'll still work?"

"Try one and see. They should be completely dry by now," he teased.

"It's the most glorious fire I've ever built, and there's no guilt in knowing its preparation was also the easiest." She headed for the kitchen. "I'd offer you wine, but we are, unfortunately, limited to our individual existences."

"I will enjoy watching you relax. Let's sit by your glorious fire and talk. You can type the words tomorrow and inject your own special spin. Tonight let's be together without your computer between us."

"Spending time together in front of a fire would be a much more romantic notion if you were visible," she said. "But I agree. I want to absorb as many facets as possible, and for tonight, I am content to just feel."

As she settled in, she said, "Nothing in me can perceive your loneliness."

They were quiet as each was lost in their own visions. "It was my personal agony. My existence lacked the same senses my body had known previously. You spend endless decades discovering your abilities and boundaries. There were rarely humans with whom to interact and I could only experiment with what was available. Over time I learned how to hear the sound of the sun, the silence of the snow."

Lively flames crackled in the stillness. Her chest ached

thinking of year upon year of the endless vacuum in which he had lived. "I can't breathe for the thought of your desolation."

"Then let's change the subject. I want you to tell me about your walks. I spent hundreds of hours exploring the cliffs and the shore. I imagine the advancements, not only with an increased population but also with technology, would make the town unrecognizable to me."

"Because the city is so old, they've preserved much of its history. You would be surprised how little has been altered."

"The first few years we were here, mother and I would make a point to walk as much of the peninsula as possible. There weren't many square feet we didn't cover."

"Do you remember the lighthouse?"

"Of course. They quit using Dyce Head the year after we built the cottage. They erected a skeletal tower just south of the original structure."

"The southern tower was destroyed a decade ago in a freak storm they call a microburst, almost the opposite of a tornado. Rather than rebuilding the new one, the city encouraged the Coast Guard to reactivate the original lighthouse, which they did. The walk along the strand is a sight I never grow tired of."

"Are there many newer buildings?"

"One of the reasons I love Castine is because it's a step back in time. The entire town is on the National Register of Historic Places, so I promise, not much has changed visually since you last strolled its streets."

"Your words please me. I will continue to envision your walks as I remember them. Thank you."

"Of course," she said. "Oh! I have an idea! I'll take videos for you on my next walk and you can see it for yourself!"

"How will you do that?"

"They don't call it a 'Smart Phone' for nothing." She grinned. "This little machine can not only record movies, it will also play them back so you can see your town."

"That boggles the mind. I would like that very much."

"Consider it done. I'm glad you thought of it."

"I didn't . . ." He chuckled when he saw her smile. "I love when you tease."

"Then I'll have to do it more often."

They sat in comfortable silence, listening to the popping sounds of aged wood, watching sparks fling themselves from the core of the heat.

"Thoroughly changing the subject again," Maisy said, "I want you to tell me the rest of your history. I've heard up until the time you were being sent overseas." She sat on the floor, glass in hand, leaning her head back against the couch.

His deep-throated laugh seemed at odds with the mood. "Ah, yes, let's turn our thoughts to more pleasant pursuits, like how I left this earthly existence and came to be here in the first place."

"Wills . . ."

"I jest. But you're going to need a lot of wine for this part. I've relived the scenes at least a thousand times. I'll do my best to keep emotion out of my accounting so you can put whatever spin you see fit in the retelling."

❧ SEVEN ❧

January 1942

"But you can't leave me." Mary Catherine was crying.

"Hush, darling." He drew her against his solid chest, kissing her hair, running his hands up her back. "I'll be back as soon as I'm able. Nothing will keep me away from you for long."

They had been married for almost two months, but Freddy was the only one who knew of their situation. The telegram had arrived that morning informing him he would ship out in two days.

How could he possibly abandon her? "Maybe I can find a way to stay."

"Of course you can't!" Her tears soaked his shirt. "You're an officer. No one gets a reprieve since Pearl Harbor, no one. You know there's no chance!"

She was wrapped tightly in his embrace. How would he be able to bear the separation? His heart was breaking. This would be the last time he would be intimate with his young bride before he would be sent overseas.

"We should tell our families."

"What do you mean?" she asked.

"Both of our families need to know we're married. I want the whole world to know, and if something happens to me . . ."

"Don't say that! Don't even think such thoughts!"

"I don't want you to be alone. I want you to have your rightful place in my family."

"But your father isn't better yet."

"It will give my mother hope – having a daughter to look out for. She always wanted one, now she has one."

"For now, Freddy knowing is enough. He can decide as time goes on how best to handle the situation. Oh, William, I can't bear the thought of losing you."

She turned in his arms and they stared at each other in the ornate mirror that hung on the bedroom wall at his cottage. "We don't have to go back until tomorrow. We'll make tonight special, one we'll always remember."

She turned her face away.

"Are you blushing?"

"I always feel like we're doing something wrong when you touch me the way you do," she said.

"Wrong? Whatever we do is perfectly acceptable between a husband and wife. All I ever want to do is bring you pleasure." His lips trailed her neck. "And you don't ever seem to mind when you lie in my arms."

Her moan was all the encouragement he needed to start their pleasurable journey to a destination known only to them.

Wills

Fall 1942

We sailed from Britain to Northern Africa as part of the Center Task Force. I was with the First Armored Division under the command of Major General Lloyd Frendenhall. He was a little man who was misplaced in his authority. He was loud and rough and made no bones about being critical of everyone with whom he came in contact, superiors and subordinates alike.

I often thought his inept leadership would bring us trouble, but I was not in a position to call him out on his faults. He constantly jumped to conclusions that were not well founded and never got involved in reconnaissance. He wouldn't listen to the recommendations of those who were familiar with the lay of the land, nor those who were more aware of the military and social conditions of the areas in which we found ourselves. So we were all relieved that the situation was quiet when we arrived in Oran, and we got our headquarters set up quickly.

Within days a shipment was delivered, and part of what finally reached us was mail from home. We all searched for a secluded place to read our letters. I had several from both my mother and Mary Catherine that had been written months earlier.

My mother's letters were full of news of how father had taken a turn for the worse soon after I'd left and she wasn't sure he was going to pull through this time. The doctors believed the problem was his heart, and having no word from me had set him back. She was trying to hold the household together, and she prayed daily for my safe return.

Mary Catherine . . . I cried when I read her words of impending motherhood. I had been gone for almost a year, so I was over the moon knowing my son or daughter had already been born. I was anxious to relieve both my mother's and my bride's worry and tell them I'd received their missives. The notion of being a father was astounding to me.

I hadn't been able to make contact with Freddy before I left. I heard he was stateside with no indication of when or where he might be deployed, but I hoped he stayed immobile so at least one of us would be near home.

I was anxious to send a telegram to my family. The letters had arrived two days earlier and there was no sign of the enemy. The past forty-eight hours had been uneventful. I located the section of town housing the telegraph office and took my lunchtime to head in that direction.

Boy or girl didn't matter, but I was consumed with wanting to watch out for Mary Catherine and holding my child in my arms. I would be the best father, and there would never be a day in my child's life when he or she wouldn't know how much their daddy loved them.

Those were the thoughts consuming me that scorching afternoon as I headed from the officers' barracks. The town was eerily still. Nothing moved, not the flight of a bird, not the air. Even the dust on the streets seemed to lie in wait for what was to happen next.

I was oblivious to the change, to an atmosphere now saturated with disaster in this small village in which we were stationed. I was single minded heading to my destination at the end of the row of whitewashed buildings. By now the heat from the tile roofs was visible in the African sun. Anxious to inform my family of my arrival, I was stopped in my tracks by a shooting pain piercing my leg.

In the few seconds it took me to become conscious of the blood soaking through my uniform, a burning agony shot through my shoulder. I saw a bright burst just before complete darkness."

Freddy

April 1945

"Sergeant Raines, Corporal Brockman is here to see you."

"Did he say what it's concerning? I'd rather not be interrupted right now."

"He said he has information about your brother, sir."

Freddy's pen stopped mid-air as his heart took on a staccato beat. "Send him in, Private." What knowledge would someone have of William?

"What can I do for you, Corporal?" Freddy asked as the young man removed his hat and stood nervously in front of the desk.

"I believe I have news of your brother, Sergeant."

"My brother's been dead for almost three years. What kind of news do you think you have?"

"I think he's alive, sir."

Freddy's heart stopped, then thundered, hardly hearing the words.

"I'm not sure, sir, but I believe I saw him in the hospital in Weimar."

"My brother is dead, Corporal."

"With all due respect, sir, I was part of Captain Raines's platoon in Oran. He was shot the week we arrived, but his body was never recovered. When the Allies liberated Buchenwald a few weeks ago, the prisoners had no identification and many were too weak to walk. They took the survivors to various hospitals."

"What makes you think my brother was among

them?"

"I was visiting one of my men in Weimar last week and thought I recognized Captain Raines. He was sleeping and, of course, emaciated, but I'm almost positive it was him."

"Have you told anyone else, Corporal?"

"No, sir. I knew you'd been transferred here and wanted to tell you directly."

"Thank you, Corporal. I will look into the situation personally. Thank you."

He saluted and left the room quietly. Freddy sat, stunned at the news. Was it possible? Was William the man he had seen?

He opened his office door. "Private, please make arrangements immediately for transport to Weimar."

"Yes, sir."

"And when you're done, find Sergeant Garrison and send him to me right away. Something urgent has come up."

"Yes, sir."

❦

Freddy stood in the doorway of the ward. Everything was white – the bed linens, the nurses' hats and uniforms and stockings and shoes, the gowns the patients wore, their faces. There were at least two dozen men scattered in beds around the huge room, but the nurse only had eyes for William. Some things never changed. Women were drawn to him as though a magic dust had been sprinkled in the air to cast a spell.

The sun was shining brightly and dancing rays ventured across William's stark-white sheets like an image in a tranquil painting. He was thrilled to see his older brother alive, but part of him was terrified. He stood for several minutes, then left without announcing his proximity. Tomorrow would be soon enough. Freddy sought out the nearest pub.

His head was throbbing the following day as he made his way to the hospital. He had no idea what he was going to do, but he'd begin by making his presence known to William.

He again stood in the doorway, observing. He watched as the patients slept, and made sure there were no nurses tending to those in their care. He crossed the highly polished floors and silently pulled up a cold seat beside the bed . . . and waited. He was in no hurry for the conversation to begin.

William's eyes opened slowly. There was a familiar smell of home. He wanted to reach it, to touch whatever was calling to him. The sun was bright and William saw the ghosts of hundreds of previous inhabitants floating across the glassy floor. He was being fanciful.

He took a few moments to let his vision adjust. Where was he? He turned his head toward the memorable smell that was drawing him, toward the man resting with his eyes closed in the metal chair next to him.

"Freddy?" His voice was weak, but the man sat up and looked back at him with the image of their uncle on his face.

"Freddy?" A lone tear escaped to the pillow.

"Hello, William." His voice was subdued.

"I can't believe you've found me! How did you know I was here? Where have you been? Were you a prisoner too? How's Mary Catherine? Mom? Dad?" His words had a hard time keeping up with the thoughts racing through his head.

"Slow down. We have plenty of time. You're not going anywhere for a while."

"How did you find me?"

"One of your men thought he recognized you when he was here visiting a friend. He sought me out to tell me."

"Oh, thank God. Thank God." He reached his hand across the crisp sheets and Freddy held it. They stared at each other for several minutes, separately lost in their own train of thought.

"You have to tell me. How is Mary Catherine? Do I have a son or a daughter?" He was holding on with his feeble strength.

"Mary Catherine has found peace, and you have a son. His name is William Andrew Raines."

He couldn't stem the flow of tears. "She named him after me. I have a son. Thank you, Freddy. And mother?"

"Mother is doing as well as can be expected." He cleared his throat. "Father died soon after they brought word you'd been killed."

"*What*?" His raised voice sent a piercing pain through his head. He quieted. "They told him I was dead?"

"You were shot the week you arrived in Oran. Your body was never found, but there was blood everywhere. The Army delivered a telegram that you were presumed dead."

"That must have been tragic for everyone. My wife who was a mother by then, my mother whose husband was sick, you."

William closed his eyes and pictured the scene unfolding at his home that dismal day. "So you've told them?"

Freddy hesitated. "No. I just found out a few days ago, and the young man who told me wasn't sure it was you. I would never have gotten their hopes up without verifying the information."

"You can send them a telegram and tell them I'm alive and well. I can't imagine the anguish Mary Catherine must have gone through."

Freddy turned away. "Dad died about a month later. Said he didn't want to live in a world without you in it." William didn't notice the anger on his brother's face.

"He didn't even want to survive to help with my son?"

"Or even his own *living* son!" Freddy pushed back the chair and paced by the side of the bed. "He acted as though his whole life was over."

After a few minutes, William said, "His attitude must have been hurtful to you. I'm sorry, Freddy."

"Oh, trust me, I was used to being second fiddle."

"It doesn't make it right."

Getting himself under control, Freddy pulled the chair back next to the bed and sat on the edge, elbows on his knees, appearing to be building up courage to say something.

"What is it? Is it mother?"

He shook his head. "No, she's fine. She mourns for you, but Willie has given her a reason to live."

"Willie? You call him Willie?" His face beamed to have a name associated with a child he had thought of for years. He pictured a younger version of himself, dimples on the lad that would charm his mother and wife. He couldn't wait to see them.

"I'm getting more able-bodied every day. Maybe I can recuperate at home when I'm well enough to travel."

Freddy stared at him for a few minutes. "Where have you been?"

"What do you mean?"

"I mean you've been gone for three years. Where have you been? Why hasn't anyone heard from you?" He had raised his voice and several heads turned their way.

William didn't want to revisit those haunting years, but needed to tell Freddy his silence had not been intentional. "I was taken prisoner the day I was shot. They didn't bother trying to fix me right away. They took me to a Dulag Luft for interrogation. After a few months of torture, they transported me to an Oflag."

Freddy shook his head, his heart clenching for what his brother must have suffered.

"They eventually allowed the Red Cross to enter and tend to our wounds, but mine had been ignored long enough there wasn't much they could do to repair the injuries."

"Where were you shot?"

"Left leg, left shoulder."

"How did you get *here*?"

"They moved us several times. The officers were treated more kindly than the enlisted men, but we were all malnourished and made to work untold hours each day. As the Allies advanced, they moved us again and again toward the interior of Germany."

He was exhausted telling the story. "Take your time."

"They would move us and taunt us with a notion of death marches. They knew most wouldn't survive. They made us walk for miles with no food, no water. Then, after several days, we arrived at the trains. Those took us to a subcamp of Buchenwald called Ohrdruf. When we disembarked, we were packed into stables like sardines. My job was to pile the bodies of my friends who died into the middle of the enclosure. There were hundreds of them."

Tears ran unheeded as he stared at the ceiling. "The thought of Mary Catherine and my child kept me sane, helped me fight to stay alive. Nothing mattered but making it home to see my family again."

"What's your prognosis?"

"I have therapy each day to help regain muscle. I can walk to the door and back, *almost* without assistance. I'm slow, but I'm getting better every day." His smile was weak. "Being able to walk unaided will take another few weeks, then I should be healthy enough to travel home. What about you?"

"What about me?"

"Where have you been?"

"I was lucky enough to stay in the states until about six months ago, and I went home often. As the Allies started to make their final push, I was sent to Germany. I have a desk job so I haven't seen combat."

"I'm so appreciative. Thank you, Freddy. Thank you for watching out for them."

He nodded. "Who knows you're here?"

"What do you mean? Just the staff."

"Have they notified the family?"

"Oh, not yet. There's too much red tape that has to be verified and proven before they can proceed. Things are more sophisticated than they were when I was imprisoned. They don't want to make more mistakes in identification."

They sat without speaking for a few minutes. Freddy stood, hat in hand, and touched his brother's shoulder. "You're worn out. I'll be back tomorrow. Don't do anything but take care of yourself in the meantime. I'll handle notifying the family."

"I love you, Freddy. I've spent years hoping you'd

survive if I didn't. I prayed daily to keep going, but somehow I knew you'd make it."

"Get some rest. I'll come see you again."

ৎৄৎৣৢৢ৾

Wills

It was April 1945, when the Allies liberated Buchenwald and the survivors were taken to Weimar. I had been excited that Freddy found me so quickly, and every time the door opened the next day, I watched with eagerness, waiting for him. He didn't show up, so when the nurses made their rounds late in the day, I accepted the sleeping pill they supplied because I was disappointed.

I was barely awake when he arrived. The sun was below the horizon, and the room had the glimmering remnants of a strange orange cast. Everyone else appeared to be asleep, but I was genuinely and sincerely happy to see him. "Hey, little brother. I waited all day for you. Didn't think you'd make it back today."

"I got here as soon as I could. I had some details I needed to figure out."

"I'm glad you're here. I hadn't seen you in years, and now twenty-four hours seems like a lifetime."

"How are you feeling?" Freddy asked.

"It's been a good day. Hoping you were coming, praying there's a chance I'll get to go home soon. The thought of being back in the States, to be able to see everyone, made me work harder during therapy."

Freddy nodded toward the sleeping patients, his crown of curly locks falling over his forehead. "Are they down for the night?"

"The nurses have already been here with our nightly meds. They normally check back about midnight, but by then everyone's sedatives have long ago kicked in, so don't expect anyone to be up partying." Talking caused me pain, but I was so thankful he was here.

"Did they give you yours?"

"Yeah, I usually take a little longer than the others, but I'll be asleep soon."

"Then I'll sit with you until it kicks in."

"Thanks." I extended my hand across the bed as Freddy pulled up a chair. Freddy rubbed his finger across my protruding veins.

"You're so frail."

"That happens when you go weeks without eating." I tried to make a joke of it.

"What was it like?"

"What was what like?" My eyes grew heavy. The medicines were running their course.

"Captivity. Being a German POW."

"It was hell. Don't want . . . to think about it."

"We need to talk."

"Not . . . going anywhere." I forced a smile and a weak squeeze. "Must have . . . been difficult for you too . . ."

After a slight pause, he said, "I can't let you come home, William."

I was sure I hadn't understood what Freddy said, but I was having such a hard time keeping my eyes open. I mustered the effort to frown, even though the words wouldn't form.

"You told me to take care of things."

I nodded but wasn't sure my muscles had actually moved my head. I squeezed Freddy's hand in acknowledgement and sympathy.

"Mary Catherine was pregnant. No one knew you were married. We hadn't heard from you in months and had no idea where you were. I didn't want to bring such shame on her, so I talked her into marrying me and telling people we had eloped and he was my baby."

I tried to get away from his painful words. Any warmth of our previous camaraderie was horribly absent. My heart pumped double time.

"How . . . could . . . you?"

Freddy shoved the chair back and paced. "Think about the reality of my situation. You had disappeared. Even before Oran we all believed you to be dead, your wife was pregnant, and I was the only one able to fix the mess you'd left us in. You should be thanking me for managing your business like I told you I would."

"No!" I wanted to scream but the word came out as a whisper.

"Then we received news you had actually died, and life was so much easier."

His words were harsh. I didn't want to listen but couldn't escape them. I wanted him to leave but had no power to tell him.

"You coming home now would ruin everything. So many men didn't return. Why weren't you one of them?"

Was this the life I had survived for? Maybe what I was hearing was the effects of the medication. Maybe I was misunderstanding what Freddy was saying.

"You've been dead for years to them. We've all gotten on with our lives. Willie thinks I'm his father. Mary Catherine loves *me* now. We have another son. We named him James. They're mine, not yours."

No pain I had suffered in the years at the hands of the Nazis came near the feeling Freddy was inflicting. I wanted to scream, to fight, to hide.

"When the telegram came of your death, father passed on shortly thereafter. When his Will was read, I hated you," Freddy said. "All that money and he had provided for Mother and left the bulk of his estate to you.

"Because you were dead, your son would have inherited your share, even before me. But no one knew you had a son except Mary Catherine and me, so the wealth came to me. As his father, I have complete control, which seems like some form of poetic justice, don't you think? No one would even suspect he's not mine, not even our mother."

Had I finally died and gone to hell? Freddy's words inflicted an unbearable agony. Why had Mary Catherine not told our son? Had I survived all these years only to find my wife was married to my brother, that they had a child together, and my own son didn't know his real father existed? What would we do? What was our solution?

"What . . . what . . ." Neither the thoughts nor words I needed would form. My arms lay abandoned at my sides like unwoven yarn.

"I've taken over the family business. I'm king of the mountain now," Freddy said. "No one even talks about you anymore except to say you were a war hero. Some hero - being captured by the enemy the week you arrived." He took pleasure in the maligning.

Freddy leaned over my face. The stench of alcohol made me want to retch. I wondered if I would suffocate if I threw up and couldn't turn my head.

"Even now, after all that time in the enemy's clutches, you still have a gaunt prettiness," he said.

All those years as a prisoner and I had held onto my sanity. In less than five minutes, he destroyed any semblance of lucidity I had.

"No sense wallowing in synthetic emotion. I can't let you come home, William. I'm sorry." His eyes were as evil as a depraved demon.

Freddy's eyes scanned the room again. He picked up a pillow from the foot of the bed and came up behind my head. I opened my eyes briefly but he wasn't there. He ran his fingers through my hair.

"I'm sorry, big brother."

The pillow came down over my face. Freddy's hands were holding it tightly on either side of my head, his full weight giving him strength. I couldn't breathe, couldn't grab air, couldn't get away. What was happening? I had to fight one more time, needed to get Freddy off me because I wanted to go home to my family. My family . . . Freddy was my family.

The scene was unfolding below me. Hate hung like venom in the air. I saw myself as Freddy continued to hold the pillow over my face. Why did he keep pressing when I wasn't even in my body?

None of this made sense. I was floating above the infirmary.

Freddy remained in that position for several more minutes, then removed the pillow from my lifeless form. He replaced the pillow at the foot of the bed and leaned over me. His ear was over my face for a while before he straightened and walked out of the room.

I kept waiting for someone to come, to notice, to sound the alarm. But it was several hours later when the nurse returned. She lifted my hand to check the pulse. I heard her gasp. I was going to tell her what happened, but when I stood beside her, she couldn't hear me.

I did everything I could think of from my lofty position to attract her attention, but she hurried out the door without being aware of my presence. Several nurses returned, poked and prodded my uninhabited body, then covered me. They wheeled me from the room and I was able to follow. No matter how loud I spoke or how near I got, I was invisible. How did they not know I was right there?"

EIGHT

June 1945

Freddy walked into the study where Mary Catherine was reading. The children were with the nanny and cook was fixing dinner.

"What is it, Freddy? You look like you've seen a ghost."

He had been back for almost a month, and their lives had settled into a peaceful routine. The next few weeks might be a small disruption, but he would finally gain the closure he craved.

"Come sit with me, darling. I need to tell you something."

"It sounds serious. Has someone died?" She had wanted to be playful, but his expression remained somber.

"You might say that."

She sat down next to him and took his hands. "What is it?"

"They've found William's body."

Her breath caught as she stiffened. "What do you mean? How do they know it's him?"

"This is the hard part. It seems he was a prisoner of war."

"Oh, no!"

"When the Allies liberated one of the POW camps, William was among the living, but just barely."

She let out a sob and pulled a handkerchief from her pocket, *crying into the soft linen. "Oh, my poor darling! Oh, God no!"*

Freddy's heart burned with white hot anger.

"He was so weak and malnourished, he didn't survive long after they rescued him. The Army has positively identified him through his dental records."

"Oh, my poor William. He was alive the whole time. How did I not know?"

He was glad he'd killed the son of a bitch. He took a deep breath to continue the story.

"They are flying his body back. It will be here in a few days. They want a ceremony to bury him with honors."

"No!" she wailed. "He wouldn't have wanted the fuss!"

"What do you mean?"

"I'm not sure your mother would survive going through a drawn out service. Let's tell her they've found his remains, but please don't share that he's been alive this whole time. It will be hard for me to be able to deal with imagining what he went through, but the reality might kill her. No ceremony. Let's lay him to rest peacefully."

"That's a wise choice, my love." He pulled her into his embrace, comforting his wife as she mourned for his brother. "No sense reopening the wounds from years ago."

"Can you imagine what he must have gone through?" Her shoulders were wracked with the force of her sobs. He held her while she cried, not for a moment regretting the decision he'd made in Weimar. When the weeping subsided, he took the handkerchief from her hand and dried her tears.

"Thank you for being such an understanding husband." She placed a kiss on his cheek. "You must be hungry. Let's go see if dinner's ready."

"Yes, Mr. Raines?"

"They're bringing my brother's body home from Germany. Will you find a few men to dig a grave by the cottage? My mother wants him buried here in the place he loved. I'll give you dimensions."

"Not a problem, Mr. Raines. When do you want us to have the plot ready?"

"The truck will bring the coffin next Saturday. There will be a small memorial, just my mother, my wife, the priest, and myself. If you will also be available afterward to close up the grave, I'll make sure you're well taken care of."

"Sure enough, we'll get right to work."

"Thank you, Reggie. There will be a small headstone to be placed later."

"Whatever you need, sir, you have only to ask."

"I knew I could count on you."

꒰ᐢ᠊ᐢ꒱

Maisy's cries interrupted his thoughts. There was a pile of tissues on the hearth and her face was red and swollen. "I had no idea," she cried. "No idea at all. What did you do?"

"There was nothing to be done at that point," he said bitterly. "In case you didn't understand, I was dead."

"Don't be an ass. Of course I understood." She was not sure she'd ever recover from Freddy's treachery.

"I read a passage once by Virginia Woolf that I've considered many times," he said. "'The beauty of the world has two edges, one of laughter, one of anguish, cutting the heart asunder.' Those were my feelings for years afterward. Up until the War, I had known only joy."

"Oh, Wills. What happened then?"

"They flew my body back and put me in the ground outside my beloved cottage. While a nation was celebrating the end of the War, I was being laid to rest long before my time. I've been here ever since."

"Did you ever see signs of remorse from him?"

"None that were evident. Life becomes easier when you learn to accept the apology you will never get."

"Did Mary Catherine know?"

"For a long time I thought she must have. But over the years of them visiting, I believe he never told anyone. He became an alcoholic, died in his fifties."

"What happened to her?"

"I have no idea. He wouldn't come back after I confronted him, and she never came back after he died."

"You confronted him? I can't wait to hear *that* story! How did you find out about his death?"

"Willie and James grew up and brought friends or spouses with them. They'd talk. One of the times they came was after Freddy's death. Said he had suffered a long and painful demise and they wanted time away."

"How long has it been since you've seen your family?"

"A long while. Donovan, one of Willie's sons, bought the place about ten years ago, then you bought it from him."

"No part of me can wrap my brain around such seclusion."

"The loneliness has been my daily agony."

His voice took on a softer tone. "One of the most exciting times of this non-existent existence was when Willie and his wife brought my grandsons. That was one of the best and one of the hardest weekends of this life."

They were in faint darkness as Maisy absorbed his

words. Her face had dried by the warmth of the fire, and the embers were all that glowed in the shadowy light.

"But you'll be pleased to know I took every available opportunity when he was here to scare him senseless. He always thought it was the alcohol, but I took perverse pleasure in playing games until he thought he was losing his mind."

Amusement flowed through her. "I'm delighted you did that."

She ran her hand over the cushions of the couch next to her for a minute. He finally had to ask, "What are you doing, my Maisy?"

"Wishing I could touch you," she said. "Wishing there was an indentation to show me you're here."

"I am right next to you. Were I a corporeal being, you would be rubbing my thigh."

She got up and crossed the room. "I'm going to sleep here tonight," she said. She lifted the hearth lid and withdrew a few logs, setting them on the dying fire. She brought a pillow and a soft, heavy blanket from her room and stretched out on the couch.

"Why?"

She hesitated in answering. "Because I don't want to be away from you. Because I feel close to you here and it's warm and comforting and I want you near."

She laid down facing the twisting flames that snapped like the dry crackle of a turning page, a tear following the same trail as so many others before. "What are we going to do, Wills?"

"What do you mean?"

"How am I ever going to let you go?"

Silence hung in the air, then her blood pounded like crashing waves as he lay down behind her.

"How did you know I was here?" he asked in a whisper as he sensed her increased pulse.

"Because my spirit hears the sound of your heart." She fell asleep almost able to feel the warmth of his arms around her.

"I'm pleased you felt the emotion of the story, Jonnell."

Maisy's route on the carpet sped up as she talked. "I have no idea when I'm going to be done. Are we working on an impending deadline?"

She listened and laughed. "Okay. I'll send you more soon."

"What did she say?" he asked as she set down her phone.

"She said there's no immediate deadline but she can't wait to read the rest so hurry up and finish." Maisy was beaming.

"I told you you could do it."

"What are you talking about? You're the one who's doing it, not me."

"I'm recounting the tale, you're threading the words together with your brilliance. The emotion is all yours. You took an idea and ran with it toward the finish line. Accept the credit due you. You're a masterful storyteller."

Their seasons together had flown swiftly and comfortably. They constantly shared and communed as Maisy's fingers flamed across her keyboard, in sharp contrast to the time when Wills had first made her aware of himself. "Okay, you need to get up and do your walk. You've skipped the past three days, I won't let you miss another."

"*You* won't let me miss? That's my decision, isn't it?"

She was teasing, but he wasn't sure.

"I would never presume to tell you what to do. You are capable and can do whatever you want. But you have missed very few days in over two years, and all of a sudden there are three in a row. I'm merely trying to encourage you."

She turned away so he couldn't see the color rise in her face.

"You think I can't see you? What's going on? There's no judgment here, just tell me."

"The other night was magical . . . our time together, your story. We've been intimately acquainted for months, but the quality of 'us' changed . . . became even more special. I can't bear the thought of being away from you for even a moment. Not only do I miss you, I've developed this insane fear you won't be here when I come back."

"For one thing, the book isn't done, so I can't leave until it's been delivered into the rightful hands."

His words were being spoken in front of her. "And for another, we might as well lay this out in the open. I've known you for years and grew to love you early on, Maisy. I hope I'm not out of line to say I believe you have similar feelings for me. I will do everything in my non-existent power to protect you." Her hands covered her face as her shoulders shook from her pain.

"But I can't dry your tears, I can't take you in my arms and comfort you. I can't run my fingers through your hair, and I can't pleasure your body. You need someone who's real, love. Someone you can share a life with. Who loves you for the dynamic woman you are, and who will treasure you until the day you die. As much as I want to be, I'm not that person."

The ache in her chest made her breath catch. "Don't,

Wills. Don't utter such nonsense. We can stay here forever. I don't mind."

"We can't, Maisy. It's not fair to you, it's not fair to me. We have a destiny we need to fulfill. You and I are merely a stopping point along the other's passageway."

The screen door slammed as she ran from the house. Ran down the trail that she knew like the back of her hand. Ran until there was little breath left in her body and her leg was burning from exertion. She collapsed on a bed of pine needles, crying until there were no more tears to be shed. She sat up, wrapping her arms around her legs, head resting on her knees.

How could she live without him? Losing him would be much worse than losing Josh. Josh – she still hadn't told Wills about her loss, her guilt. She needed to explain. Brushing debris from her clothes, she headed back to the house at a much slower pace than how she'd left.

"Thank God. I was afraid you wouldn't come back."

"You never have to worry about that eventuality. You have my word. I don't have the courage to leave you, so if there's ever going to be a separation, you're the one who will have to be strong enough. Since you're currently bound here, I'm pretty confident I'm not in imminent danger."

"Maisy . . ."

"Don't. Let me live in this life we have for now. I will savor each moment and feel all I can while we're together. I'm going to soak in a tub, then we're going to have another night of sharing. I'm ready to tell you what happened with Josh. I admire how you've gotten past your betrayal because I haven't found that graciousness yet, but I find healing in you. It's time."

The cool gusts of wind announced the coming of autumn. The leaves were changing and the evening temperatures were getting colder. The lapping flames of the fire cast a welcoming glow in the otherwise dim room. "I love spending time here when there's no light except from the fireplace. It's intimate, and somehow the dark gives me the courage to be honest."

"Thank you for trusting me enough."

"How could I not? You've shown me every day how well you take care of me. I need to do this."

"It will help you to let go of it."

"I know. I think sharing will be cathartic. One of the reasons I was able to tell your story the way I did was because I related to it. Of course I will never understand exactly what you suffered, but betrayal was at the core of my heartache too."

"I'm sorry you've had such painful circumstances. Life is often unfair."

"I feared for so long you would judge me if you knew the truth – about Josh, about Traci, about the accident. I love you enough I'm ready to take that chance. I want to be free of this burden."

"Nothing you can say or do can change my feelings for you."

"But you're still going to leave me."

"You are so important to me, I want someone who can satisfy not only your heart, but all of your worldly needs as well. The fact is, while I don't understand the process, it's not my choice to make."

"Don't make me cry. I don't want to cry right now."

"Then sit. I'm listening."

The rug felt soft to the touch as she sat on the floor again, head relaxed against the couch, resting her eyes.

"I'm right here with you, Maisy. My legs are around you and I'm running my fingers through your hair. You have nothing to fear. You're safe, and loved beyond measure."

His words gave her comfort and security.

Maisy

"You look beautiful tonight, Mrs. Hollis," Josh had said. I can still hear him as though it was yesterday.

"Thank you." I didn't know why I was blushing. We were celebrating our fourth anniversary, but I wasn't used to him complimenting me or being effusive. Paying me undivided attention was not his habit and made me uncomfortable.

"Would you like dessert?" the server asked, interrupting my irreverent thoughts.

"No, I'm fine," I said. I wanted him to bring our check so we could get out of there.

"I'd like another glass of wine," Josh said. He raised my hand to his lips. My eyes flew to the waiter almost desperately. He promptly took his leave.

"I was so blessed the day I found you," Josh said.

"We were in third grade. It was hardly magical fireworks." I was trying to divert the awkward situation.

"There's always been something about you – something special. So dynamic."

He rubbed my fingers as though they held answers for him. "Margaret, I'm so fortunate that you're my wife." He wasn't looking at me and I almost laughed. He seemed so sincere and so disingenuous at the same time.

"Just how much *have* you had to drink?" I teased. "I had half a glass and you polished off the rest of the bottle."

"Why would you ask me that?" His voice was loud and he sounded angry.

Something was off and he was making me uncomfortable.

"Because you're acting strangely."

"Is it strange to tell my wife that her hair is the color of sunshine on a wheat field before harvest?" His voice was still slightly raised.

This time I did laugh.

"When you've rarely complimented me before, it's a little disconcerting."

"Today's our anniversary. There shouldn't be anything abnormal about me admiring the most desirable woman in the room."

The waiter set the glass in front of him. "Will that be all?"

"Yes, we'll take the check, please."

"Of course, ma'am."

Josh turned back toward me. "I can't wait to get you home." He finished the entire drink in a few swallows.

I studied the face of my husband, this person who had been part of my life for almost two decades, but tonight I didn't seem to know him at all. If I'm going to be honest, our relationship had its ups and downs and had become somewhat boring lately, as Josh liked to remind me daily. But nothing was ever too harsh that we hadn't gotten past our difficulties, or that we wouldn't get past now. But this was a side of him I had never seen. My normally laid-back husband was intense and almost frightening.

"What's going on, Josh?"

"What do you mean? Nothing's going on. Why would you accuse me of something like that?"

His agitation got my attention. "Accuse you? Accuse

you of something like what?"

"What's going on in your brain? Let's get out of here," he said, throwing bills on the table and taking my hand to lead me out of the subdued, upscale restaurant.

As though remembering a plan, he slowed down, drew my fingers to his lips, and pulled me to him. "I'm sorry, baby, let's not fight. I've had this night planned for weeks." His breath reeked and I was almost afraid.

I had no idea what was wrong with him, but his behavior was disturbing enough I wanted to find out before we got home. There was a wrought-iron swing along the sidewalk leading to the restaurant. As we passed, I took a seat, stopping Josh in his tracks.

"What are you doing? Come on!" he said, trying to pull me with him.

"Sit down." I patted the space next to me, wanting to buy some time. "You've had enough to drink that we can wait a few minutes. Come, tell me what's going on."

"Why do you keep insinuating something's going on?" He had raised his voice and was sounding belligerent.

I tugged gently and he plopped onto the open space next to me. "We have all the time in the world and I'm a patient woman. There's nothing we can't talk about, and I'm in the mood to listen."

I was turned away from him when his body began shaking. "Tell me what's wrong." I grew genuinely alarmed when I took his chin and turned his face toward me. "Josh, what happened?"

He threw his arms around me, the stench of alcohol made me queasy. "Tell me. It can't be all that bad."

"I'm going to have a baby!" he wailed.

The vision of a pregnant Josh had me giggling until the reality of what he said sank in. We had tried for years to conceive, something we both wanted. My inability to get pregnant had been a nagging source of private shame, and over time we had given up on our dream.

"*Who?*"

"Traci."

Numbness like I'd never experienced washed over me. Traci?

"Not *my* Traci?' I asked. My dearest friend and my husband? Before there was Josh, there was Traci. Best friends in kindergarten. Best friends now. No, not now.

"*My* Traci?"

"Oh, Margaret, I'm so sorry. I never meant for it to happen. Neither of us wanted to hurt you. You were gone to your convention for a few days, she dropped some stuff at the house, and one thing led to another." His weeping turned to pleading.

"You have to believe me, I've never loved anyone like I love you."

His words encouraged chaos in me. My scattered brain furiously grabbed at pieces, trying to fit them nicely together before they crumbled and destroyed me. "I haven't been to a convention since last winter, almost fifteen months ago. You've been seeing each other this whole time?"

How could I not have seen the signs? Suspected? How had they kept their relationship a secret from me?

The metal joints shrieked a cacophony of warning. The rhythm of the swing punctuated my thoughts. "This whole time? Over a year?"

"I wanted to stop, I swear I did. I went months without seeing her and then we couldn't help ourselves. I'm so sorry." I jerked away when he pulled me into his arms. I sat frozen.

"How far along?"

"Almost three months. I tried to convince her to have an abortion, but she wouldn't hear of it."

"You've talked about having kids as long as I've known you. Why would you even think about talking her into that?"

"Because you're what I want. I was afraid you'd find out as she got bigger. She threatened to tell you. But I don't want her, I want you. I'm *so sorry*."

I didn't move, chillingly numb as I thought back to three months ago. "You were together when I went to Augusta to help my mom when Daddy had a heart attack?"

"Stop it! Don't do that to yourself, to us."

He had been so solicitous while I was away. I thought back to all the times he'd called. How sweet he'd been to me. His concern was all a lie.

"Say something. Please, Margaret, say you'll forgive me."

Falling raindrops made me mindful of my surroundings and moved me to action. I stood, pulled my keys from my purse and dashed toward the car.

"Where are you going?" He ran behind me, grabbing my arm as I pushed the fob to unlock the car.

"Home."

"Then you'll forgive me? We'll get past this? Oh, thank you." He took my hand. "I knew you'd understand." I was wet and shaking when I got behind the wheel so I fumbled as I buckled my seat belt and started the car.

I could see the moment he realized I was going to drive away, so he ran to the passenger side. God forgive me, I even thought of accelerating as he passed in front of the car. He didn't even have time to close the door as I sped up to merge into traffic. "You will forgive me, won't you, Margaret?" I suddenly hated hearing my name come from his lips.

"Not in this lifetime."

Silence. His body stiffened. "What do you mean?"

"I have no intention of sticking around for the conclusion of this sordid little fairy tale. By the time your child is born, your divorce will be final. You'll be one little happy family."

"*No!*"

His voice was so jarring I jerked my head in his direction. His face was splotchy, the veins standing out on his temples.

"You will not leave! I won't allow it! I don't want a future with Traci!"

"It's a little late to decide that." The smell of alcohol was stifling inside the car. I hoped to make it home before I threw up, but my queasiness wasn't just from the stench.

"I'll not spend another night in your house, Josh."

My overriding thought was to get home, pack a bag, and get away from the nightmare my life had become in the last fifteen minutes.

"It's *our* house! You're not going anywhere." He grabbed my shoulder. "Do you hear me?"

"I'd be hard pressed not to. Take your hand off me. I'm doing fifty-five and it's pouring rain, and there's nothing to talk about. If you think I'll stick around and watch my former best friend give birth to my husband's bastard love child, you're grossly mistaken."

He was quiet for a moment, then shrieked in rage, "Why wouldn't I want to sleep with someone who wasn't a cold fish like you, you *bitch*?" I saw stars from an impact that blindsided me.

❧ NINE ❧

July 1949

"Hello, Willie."

"Hello. Who are you?"

"My name is William, too."

"Where are you?"

"If you look in the mirror you'll be able to see me."

The young boy climbed on the chair. "Are you my grandfather?"

The man in the mirror laughed. "No, but I look like him, don't I?"

"You look like a picture my grandmother has of him at her house. He died right after I was born."

"I'm very sorry to hear that. What are you doing inside all by yourself?"

"My brother and I were playing and I got to be the Indian. He wanted my feathers instead of his cowboy hat and I didn't want him to. My initials are on it and I don't want to share."

"Will you show me?"

He brought the headdress from behind his back that William's mother had so painstakingly made for him when he was the same age. But that wasn't something the young lad *would understand.*

"That's a fine headpiece you have. Someone once told me that even though your initials spell WAR, you must always try to live at peace with everyone."

"What do you mean?"

"It will make more sense when you're a little older. Would you like to find a hiding place so, no matter what, your brother will never be able to find it?"

"You bet I do!"

"Then hurry. We probably don't have much time before someone comes in. Go into your parent's bedroom and I'll tell you where."

The precocious youth climbed down and ran into the adjoining room. "You'll need to stand on the bench under the window," Wills explained. "Do exactly as I tell you, and you mustn't ever tell anyone about what I'm about to show you. Promise?"

"I promise. I'm real good at keeping secrets."

"I'm proud of you, Willie, now listen carefully."

When the deed was done and Willie was running to the back door, he turned. "Who are you, mister?"

"Someone who loves you very much."

The young boy's brow furrowed, and he was gone in a flash, on his exuberant way.

"**M**aisy. I'm here," Wills said. "You're safe. There's nothing you're seeing that isn't there when the lights are on. Nothing can hurt you. Take your time."

She heard his words but she was lost in the past, her mind racing to the next memory.

Maisy

Someone was squeezing my hand. There was an excruciating agony in my leg but I was immobile.

"Wake up, darling, can you hear me?"

My brain was foggy. Was that my mother's voice? I strained to hear but moving hurt. Where was I? Every part of my body was in pain. I tried to say something but was too tired. I drifted back to sleep.

"Can you wake up, Magnolia? Traci's here to see you."

How strange. My mother hadn't called me Magnolia in years. And what was Traci doing here? She was supposed to be out of town for a few weeks. But I didn't want to entertain anyone, and I sure didn't feel like talking. I feigned sleep. All I wanted was to be alone.

"She's awake! She opened her eyes!"

The light streaming through the window was blinding. Where was I? Why was my mother here? It took a moment for my eyes to adjust. I was in a room I didn't recognize.

"Mom?"

"Oh, darling, you're awake!"

"And that's cause for excitement?"

The effort of speech caused throbbing in my head. "God, where am I? Why do I hurt like this?"

My father stepped to the edge of the bed, a tear standing in his eye, falling as he exchanged a look with my mother. "Welcome back, Munchkin." He squeezed my hand. I don't think I flinched, but I felt injured.

"Where have I been?" I thought I was making a joke, but no one else seemed to think I was funny.

My father took a seat across the room. Mother looked away. "There was an accident."

"What kind of accident?"

"A car accident. Don't you remember?"

I tried to grab a thought, a memory, but nothing felt familiar. "When was that?"

"Nine days ago," my mother said softly.

"What are you talking about? Where have I been?"

"Right here. You've been in a coma. We didn't know when you'd wake up."

My eyes toured the hospital room, but the effort was too wearying. My leg was in a cast, suspended from the bed with a wire.

Being disoriented was easier to deal with. I went back to sleep.

Someone was crying. Sounding like a chalkboard screech, all I wanted was for whomever was making that god-awful noise to stop. I swam to the surface of consciousness, hoping to make them go away. The blonde sitting next to the bed appeared to be the source of the discord. Traci? Why was she wailing like that? The racket was unsettling.

"Don't cry, please." I wasn't trying to be sympathetic, I wanted her to be quiet.

"Meggie! You're awake."

Why was her presence so grating? Didn't she know I wanted to be alone? I didn't want to appear rude, so I said, "Yeah, that's me, awake and ready to party." It took so much effort to say even that sentence.

"I'm so sorry. Oh, Meggie, I'm so, so sorry."

The crying started again and I didn't care if I was impolite or not. Dear God, I needed her to shut up.

Turning toward Traci, I had the less-than-charitable thought that she'd put on weight. Funny, she even appeared to be pregnant. Pregnant. My brain was swimming. Pregnant? Had I known Traci was pregnant?

I searched my foggy brain for the answer. The memory of my anniversary night came flooding in like a tidal wave. Traci *was* pregnant.

"Get out." I was unable to scream, unable to express my anger, but I wanted this woman who had been my best friend for decades to get out of my sight.

"What?"

"Thank God, at least your incessant wailing has stopped. I said get out and don't come back. Ever."

"Margaret Marie! What's gotten into you?" My mother and father were coming in the room.

"Traci, I'm sorry. She doesn't know what she's saying. She's been so medicated . . ."

"I know good and damn well what I'm saying. For the last time, get out and don't come back. I'll take out a restraining order if you come here again." It was probably the first time my parents had ever heard me swear, but none of our lives would ever be the same. This was just the beginning.

"Margaret! Traci has been here every day since your accident, sitting by your side, holding your hand, heart broken for you."

Mother turned toward Traci. "Please forgive her. She's been through so much."

"Don't you dare apologize for me! Her tears were for herself, not me. When you get her out of here, put a sign on the door that I'm not to have visitors except for you and Daddy."

My father walked to my bedside and touched my arm

as my mother walked Traci to the door.

"I'm so sorry," Traci said, sniveling again. "I'm so sorry."

"Yeah, tell it to someone who cares," I said, hoping she'd hear my weak voice.

"It's all right, dear, she'll come around. You'll see," my mother said.

I closed my eyes. I'd never come around, but there was no sense arguing with my mother. Time would prove the point.

Wills' voice penetrated her reverie. "Take a break, Maisy. Do you want another glass of wine?"

"No. I'm all right. I want to finish." She put more wood on the dying fire. "Thank you, but if you can stand to listen, really, I'm fine." She sat back down.

"Then continue. I'm right here."

Several days passed and each one brought continued healing, along with a new clarity and drive. A week after I'd kicked Traci out, my mother and father pulled up chairs next to my bed. My father cleared his throat.

"What's going on?" I looked between my parents and my favorite nurse, Ellie, who was standing in the doorway.

"You haven't asked about Josh," my mother began.

"He's wise to keep his distance."

"What do you mean?" My father was squeezing my hand.

"I mean I don't want to see him. He knows I'd kick him

out if he showed up, so I'm glad he's stayed away."

Mother and father exchanged a look. Ellie stood at my shoulder.

"Margaret," father said.

"Josh is dead," my mother finished.

"*What?*"

"He died in the accident. He wasn't wearing a seat belt and was thrown from the car. He died . . . he died that night."

I had never thought to ask about him. I knew I was glad he hadn't been visiting. But dead? Josh was dead? Is that why Traci had been grieving by my bedside every day?

"Why didn't you tell me before?"

"The doctors told us to wait until you were more stable, or to tell you when you asked. You never asked, and we're so sorry, Margaret. This must come as a horrible shock."

I tried to process what this news meant to me. I wasn't sure. A lone tear escaped to trail down the side of my face. I closed my eyes. "Would you mind leaving me alone for a while? Thank you for telling me. I need some time."

"Are you sure . . ."

"I'm positive. Thank you, but I want you to go now."

Ellie led them to the door. My mother hesitated. "He loved you so much. I don't know what happened, but you were his whole life."

I didn't respond.

When the door shut behind them, I opened my eyes. I thought back to that night and remembered our anniversary celebration. I remembered the dinner and the strange way he'd been acting.

And I remembered our conversation on the swing. But

no matter how hard I tried, I had no memory of what happened afterward. Didn't remember going to the car, wasn't even sure which one of us had been driving although I knew I wouldn't have let Josh drive. He'd been too drunk and I wouldn't have gotten in a car with him.

Was the accident my fault? Had we argued? I didn't remember. I wasn't sure I wanted to.

Depression weighed on my shoulders like a heavy winter coat. The dampness on my cheeks surprised me. I was crying, something I hadn't done in a long time. The floodgates opened and wrenching sobs tore through me. Someone put a tissue in my hand.

"Let it all out, darlin'. You'll feel much better."

"I was leaving him, Ellie. It was our anniversary and I was leaving him. But I don't remember what happened, not at all, and I'm trying very hard to be sorry."

Ellie was silent, processing what she'd heard. I was not only her patient but we had become friends. She stood by me as I continued to weep.

"He was having an affair with my best friend and told me on our anniversary that she was pregnant but he still wanted to be married to me."

Ellie hesitated. "Was that your friend Traci?"

I nodded as anger replaced sorrow.

"The doctor ordered a sedative to help you sleep. Let me know if you want it."

I answered immediately. "Yes, please. I don't want to think any more tonight."

"The lack of memory is normal. Often when you have a concussion, you don't remember what happened right before the blow. It may or may not ever come back, but don't strain yourself chasing to catch the memory. Something might trigger it someday . . . or not."

The next five months I healed, learned to walk again, gained strength, and reflected on what my life had turned into. Some days I wondered why I worked so hard to be whole. Some days I was determined to become the famous writer Josh always told me would never happen.

Josh . . . I made an effort to not think about him. There's no question our marriage was over the night of our anniversary, but how long before then had we *really* ceased to have a relationship and I had been too stupidly blind to not see?

Time and physical pain allowed me to get to a point of forgiveness for both Josh and Traci. I didn't want to have a relationship with her, but I had forgiven her because it was something I needed to do for myself.

Ellie was invaluable during my convalescence - encouraging me, always there for me, telling funny stories, listening. She spoke often of the town on the shore where her family had spent their summers. A sparsely populated city about an hour away sounded magical. I would get on the internet daily and read about Castine, and dream how idyllic life would be away from the hustle of what I'd always known, an escape to be alone and write.

When I was released from the hospital, the thought of ever going back to the house I'd shared with Josh was abhorrent, so I sold it, much to my parent's chagrin. No amount of cajoling would induce me to spend another night in what had been our house. He had indicated at least one of his trysts had been there, and I would have been foolish to not believe many others had been as well. I wouldn't dwell on those images, but there was no need to take that walk down memory lane and be plagued with those kinds of pictures in my head.

With the proceeds from the sale of our house and his insurance policy, I was able to purchase Summerset. If I was frugal, I had enough to survive for years, which would give me time to see if I could succeed as an author.

Traci came by my parent's house several times to see me. When I left town, the time was near for Josh's child to be born. I didn't want to hear about celebrations, didn't want to know its name, wanted nothing to do with their baby. My life with them was behind me, and I was not going to wait around to tear open that raw wound again.

My parents were heartsick I was moving but I'd be less than an hour away, and I was anxious to escape the memories and pain of being there. I had to promise I'd come home often. All of my worldly possessions now fit in my car, and I left with no remorse. I stayed at a Bed and Breakfast on Penobscot Bay for two days until my new furniture arrived to help me begin my new life.

᠅

As Maisy took a break, Wills said, "You cannot possibly understand how excited I was for your new life to begin either. Sarah showed up one day and started cleaning. Then the truck delivered your furniture and you were directing traffic, and I thought I'd finally died and gone to heaven."

"Because someone was moving in?"

His voice was low, seductive. "And because I thought you were one of the sexiest cookies I'd ever seen. It's not inappropriate for me to say that now, is it?"

"Trust me, you can tell me anytime, and anything else that strikes your fancy. No matter how old fashioned your words," she teased, "it make my heart sing knowing you feel the way I do."

"But nothing has affected me in almost a century," he continued, "like the day you brought home the mirror and stripped off your clothes by the front door."

Maisy gasped and threw a hand over her mouth. "Oh, my God!" They were both laughing. "I was so proud of myself for having the courage to do that! Never in my life had I ever been as daring. So much for the confidence you experience when you think you're alone."

"I viewed your actions as those of a self-assured woman. The freedom that allowed you to be that secure in yourself was some sort of victorious right of passage. At that moment I knew, if I had a heart, it would belong to you."

His words made her sorrowful. "Let me finish my story because I don't want to wait and have it hanging over my head another day." But his understanding and compassion had healed so many bruises to her soul.

Maisy

The first month I was here was like a dream come true. I was so happy I got to set up house the way I wanted. We were so young when we got married and I had deferred to Josh and how he wanted things to be arranged. 'Clutter' is the word that best describes all he touched. For a man so fastidious in dress, his hoarding made me crazy.

His parents and my parents and our grandparents had given us enough to furnish our first place. I found the too-many, mismatched pieces stifling, but Josh would never let me get rid of anything, and I hadn't wanted to rock the boat.

When I got here, I painted my kitchen yellow, a color

Josh hated, and decorated brightly but sparsely. I bought comfortable but sterile furniture, and used cheerful paint and pillows throughout rather than overrunning it with knick-knacks.

After I'd been here for a few weeks, I woke up from a nightmare. I was in so much pain and no position would relieve the throbbing. I moved to the living room couch and threw my leg over the back, which eased the ache somewhat.

In that state between wakefulness and sleeping, drifting in and out of sleep, the nightmare came. I woke but didn't move, on one hand afraid I might catch the foggy thread but wanting to face whatever was looming in the darkness.

Josh and I had been arguing in the car. The rain was pouring and it was hard to see so I was concentrating on the road. He was drunk and wasn't wearing a seatbelt. That's a belt they have in cars that is used to strap you to your seat.

I was insisting to him that I wouldn't stay and he hit me. A bright light flashed in my head, whether from his fist or something else I'll never know.

Our car slammed into a concrete road divider and spun, flipping several times down an embankment. When we came to rest, Josh wasn't in the car and I was hanging upside down in the storm. I was shrouded in wet blackness. I was still strapped in, but my head was at an awkward angle because I was against the roof, and my leg was twisted in an unnatural position.

I had no idea where my phone was, but I called out to Siri as though she was a lifeline and I told her to dial nine-one-one. That was the last thing I remembered until I woke up in the hospital with my parents by my side more than a week later.

❦

Maisy cried in anguish at the memory. Regardless of his indiscretions, she would never have wished death for him. He was so young, so full of life. She was wracked with guilt.

"It wasn't your fault, sweetheart," Wills reassured her. "Please don't blame yourself. Not now, not ever."

"Thank you. I understand that truth in many levels of my brain. The memory of that night is excruciating. First finding out about the betrayal by the man I'd known and loved most of my life, and then his death. Was I responsible?"

"Don't go there, don't let your mind dwell on blame. There was nothing you could have done to prevent the outcome. The accident wasn't your fault."

"You're right, but sometimes I have doubts. That night as I lay on the couch and remembered, I cried for at least an hour before I gave in to a fitful sleep. I was exhausted as the sun came through the windows and crawled across me. Ellie had been right. Remembering added no benefit to my healing except possible closure."

Maisy

The next morning my mother called and woke me up. My neck hurt from how I'd been sleeping and I was emotionally spent. I wasn't in the mood to talk to anyone and certainly wasn't in the mood to be pleasant, but I didn't want to take my bad disposition out on her so I tried to be friendly. "Yes, ma'am?"

"Good morning, sweetheart. How are you doing?"

"I'm loving my little cottage, Mom. You're up awfully early. What's up?"

"Margaret . . ." Uh oh, I knew that tone of voice and I wasn't going to like whatever came next.

"Margaret, Traci came by yesterday."

"I don't care. I don't want to see her or hear about her."

"Margaret, she brought her baby, her son. She wants so desperately to heal what happened between you. Won't you give her another chance?"

I refused to engage in the conversation.

"It might help if you talked to her. She's hurting as much as you are at the loss of your friendship, and she's broken hearted because you've lost your husband and won't let her comfort you."

"Please make this the last time we have this discussion. Nothing will make me change my mind."

"But, Margaret, you don't understand. You've been friends most of your lives. She's grieving with you. She loves you so much she even named her son after your husband."

I was stunned. Her words swirled in my foggy brain. "What did you say?"

"She named her son Joshua Adam after Josh. Wasn't that the kindest gesture?"

"Kind, Mother? Kind? She named her son after his father. You're a better person than I am if you can find the *kind* in her betrayal."

¿ᢙᒍᔐᑊ

"I remember that morning well," Wills said. "I had no idea what was going on, but I wanted so much to wrap my arms around you. I saw how upset you were with the conversation."

"Thank you. You're absolutely right. I was shaking I was so angry. Then the phone rang again. I refused to answer. I didn't care how shocked she was at what I'd said, at least now they'd know the truth. When the phone rang yet again, I left it to vibrate on the table. I put on my jacket and headed out for an early walk. There weren't enough miles to cover on this peninsula to rid myself of the outrage I felt at the audacity Traci had to claim Josh's name. I didn't wish ill on her, but she sure didn't seem like the girl who had been my friend all my life.

"Part of me felt I hadn't moved far enough away to separate myself from the memories and the pain of betrayal. Initially I regretted having told my mother. I never wanted to explain the details to her, and I was afraid I'd have to recount the whole sordid mess. But then I decided to let my mother put two and two together and come up with whatever answer she wanted. She didn't have to know the details, just the results. That was enough."

"Maisy, I wish you felt my arms around you. I wish you understood my feelings for you."

She was exhausted and laid down on the couch, eyes closing.

"It makes perfect sense now," he said.

"What does?"

"Your inability to complete the first story. You'd pitched the idea to Jonnell before you knew about Josh and Traci, correct?"

"Long before. When I wrote the outline it was interesting, which is why they bought the rights in the first place. Until it hit too close to home. After the accident, I couldn't take myself out of the story enough to finish."

"You're going to give them something much better."

She hugged herself, imagining she could feel him. "Don't leave me, Wills. I need you. You were gone decades before I met you, but you're the most important part of my world."

Something in him broke at her words.

❧ TEN ❧

August 1950

"Mama said to tell you the car's all packed." Willie had been keeping his distance, but he'd been watching his father tear the place apart for the last ten minutes.

"Tell her I'll be out when I'm done."

"What are you doing?"

"None of your business!" His father continued his search.

"Can I help?"

"No. I'm trying to find something of your grandmother's. We've looked everywhere and I thought maybe she left it here."

"What is it?"

"An old sapphire ring. She wore it all my life. Just some sentimental value, that's all."

"*I*'m not exactly sure how to end the story, Jonnell. I'm going to take some time to gather options."

He was standing beside her, trying to determine what

this was about.

"Of course I won't take years, silly. I'm trying to decide what the most favorable outcome would be. Sure, I'll call you in the next few days, don't worry."

"What's going on?" he asked.

"Nothing."

"Maisy, it's me, remember? I know you. Tell me what's going through your brain."

"I'm going for a walk. I'll be back soon."

"Please, talk to me. Don't leave." The door banged behind her.

Her teeth were chattering when she came into the house a while later. "It's a lot colder out there than I thought."

"If I were able, I'd draw you a hot bath. As it is, I'll request you start one for yourself before you catch your death of cold."

"That's an antiquated notion. But yes, master. At your service, master."

"Tell me what's happening to you."

"Let me warm up, Wills. We'll talk later."

She was tying the fluffy robe around her waist and tidying up after suffering through a long night.

"Tell me, love. I can't help if I don't know what's going on in your head."

"We've been working at breakneck speeds. I thought taking time off might be a good idea. Have you ever been acquainted with the concept of slowing down?"

"Why would we do that?"

"Seriously? You can seriously ask me that?"

"I just did. What has you so bothered?"

"Why do you keep asking me that? Don't you have

something you want to show me to prepare us for winter? Every day I can feel the temperature drop. We should probably be planning."

He chose to let her reluctance slide for now. She was dealing with a problem he didn't understand and he'd give her a little more time.

"You're going to be so impressed. Short of dropping them on your head, I couldn't figure out how to tell you about the shutters." His laugh eased her mood.

"This sounds like we're going to have an adventure. Let me get a cup of coffee and throw on some clothes. You'll wait for me, won't you?"

"Very funny."

She came out of her room buttoning a sweater. "Wills?"

"I'm here."

"Thank you."

"For what?"

"For letting me spill my guts. For listening. I'm trying to process where the pieces fit in my brain, but something's different. The memory doesn't feel like so much of a threat. Thinking about them can't hurt me anymore and those incidents are part of what allowed me to get to the point where I am now. I'm here and I'm getting healthier by the day. Most importantly, I survived. Thank you for helping me fit those shards together."

"I'd move heaven and earth for you if such a talent was in my power."

"No need. Show me where the shutters are instead. I can't wait."

Her mood was more upbeat. Maybe that's all that had been wrong.

"Okay, open the windows so you can hear what I'm

saying. Get a rag and a flashlight, then you can step outside."

The front of the house faced the water and had been well maintained over the years, protecting the decking and the siding from the elements. She loved sitting on the porch, rocking in her traditional wicker rockers, and was surprised with all the time she'd spent out here that there might be a hiding place she didn't know about.

"The light to the right of the door – grab the fixture and push to the right."

"The whole fixture?"

"Whatever kind of grip you need to move the light to the side. The opening will be swollen from decades of not being used, but consider the sconce like a door to a closet and push or pull as necessary to unstick the frame from the wall."

It took several minutes for the brass lantern fixture to give way. She pulled slowly, having no idea what she'd find inside. She turned the flashlight beam into the opening and her grin broadened.

"I'm intrigued. There are a lot of spider webs and two long, metal handles sitting on the bottom."

"Use the rag to wipe away the webs, then pull the crank handles out."

When she was done, he said, "Attach them to each other and insert the longer end into the slot in the back. The prongs should lock into place."

"Got it."

"Now turn the crank slowly. You should be able to grip the shaft with both hands for an easy movement."

As she made several revolutions of the handle, a sound above her head startled her and she stopped abruptly.

"You probably should have waited until after we did

this to take your shower. I'm sorry I didn't realize sooner. There's nothing in the noise that's going to harm you, but after all these years, you're going to get dirty, so be prepared."

She turned with a new sense of adventure when all of a sudden the roof appeared to be falling. She let out a gasp, fearful the ceiling would fall on her head.

"The ledge is moving exactly as intended. You're not going to be hurt."

"If you say so, boss." She continued to crank.

The entire covering of the porch pivoted down away from the house. She cranked faster until it wouldn't lower further. On the shelf were six shutters, two deep.

"There are twelve windows around the house, and there should be twelve shutters," he said.

"There are."

"Good. They're simple to attach and they shouldn't be too heavy. My father made them with my mother in mind in case she ever had to install them when he wasn't here, so I'm hoping they're not too cumbersome for you."

She lifted one down. "No problem here. I can handle the weight easily."

"He built them to slip on and off without much effort, but when we secured the place at the end of each season, he always put them on and left them. If you're living here, you'll probably only want them on in the deep of winter."

It was obvious how they attached at the top and she hooked the first one on the window.

"Good girl. Each shutter has a number carved into its side – one through twelve. The window closest to the fixture is window one. They progress from there."

She took the second one down. "Each window casing has a rod at the bottom. The shutters either hook to the eye of the rod, or you can extend them to hold the shutter open if you want air flow or sunshine when they're in place."

"Brilliant!"

"That's how I always felt about my father. He had simple but ingenious ideas."

"I'm thrilled these are here. There have been times in the winter when the wind blew so hard off the Bay I was sure the force of the gusts would shatter the glass."

"This will keep the house warmer, too, and you shouldn't have to use so much electricity."

"Ah, yes, you would have heard me complaining."

"Yes, but I didn't know how to solve the problem for you. Now you will be able to tend to it."

She replaced the shutters in their resting place and cranked the ceiling back. "You were right," she said, stepping into the living room, "I'm going to need another shower. Creepy crawly creatures in my wet hair gives me the jitters."

"I'm proud of you."

"For what? Following directions?" She paused. "I want to hug you and thank you for taking care of me. I appreciate you."

"It's my pleasure. As much as I want to provide for you, I will be satisfied that you can take care of yourself when I'm gone."

"Stop saying that!"

"If we lose sight of our goals we'll both be held prisoner. You'll love an apparition and I will always regret I prevented you from finding what you need."

"Don't you understand? I don't need any more than what I have. I'm as happy and content as I've been in my entire life."

"You need a flesh and blood man who can take you in

his arms and love you the way you should be loved, not a ghost who can't even dry your tears."

"Stop telling me what I need!"

She slammed the door as she went to take another shower.

She took her time. When she came out she fixed herself a cup of tea and sat at the table and read emails.

"We can't ignore this forever," he said.

"Wanna bet?"

His immediate rumble of laughter tickled her. "I'll make a deal with you, Maisy. We won't talk about what's to come until the time draws nearer. When the book's done, we'll think about what happens then."

"Whatever," she said, putting her cup in the sink and walking out the door.

When she returned, he said, "I kinda like this surly side of you. It makes me want to turn you over my knee and . . . sorry. What I want to do to you is probably best left unsaid as well."

"What are we going to do, Wills?"

"What we have to do. You're going to write a book that will put you on the map. You're going to follow your dream and let the world know how amazing you are."

She looked out the open window, the fresh, crisp smell of salt water tiptoeing through the room as a gentle breeze stirred. She rubbed her arms, silent tears falling.

"What is it, love? What's going on in your mind?"

"If I finish, you'll be gone. I can't be the cause of losing you."

He was quiet for a few minutes. So this was the issue. "I spent the last years of my earthly life as a prisoner of war of a cruel and deranged monster. There were few bright spots in a world shrouded in death and sorrow. The thought of home kept me going and wanting to heal from the atrocities man was capable of inflicting upon his fellow man, only to have someone in my family take that very life."

Her head was bowed, grieving his circumstance.

"Now I'm in a different kind of prison I don't understand. But an indisputable fact is that you're a beacon of light in three-quarters of a century of darkness. I'd give my life to be able to hold you, but I don't have a life to give. I want my freedom so you can have your freedom and not squander the life I'd give anything to share with you. Can you understand?"

Sobs racked her. She collapsed to the couch and cried until her head ached and her throat was sore. They were passionately at odds with no visible solution. She was asleep within minutes, small hiccoughs punctuating her breathing.

When she awoke, she sat up slowly. "Wills?"

"Yes, my love."

"Oh, Wills."

"I know, sweetheart."

They didn't talk for a time. "I don't have the courage to do what you're asking of me for myself." She took a tissue and dried her face. "But I love you enough I'm willing to pursue this for you. I'm not sure how I can survive, but I'll do whatever you need."

"You have nerve you don't even know you possess. But for the time we have, let's have fun finishing this story and see what life has on the horizon."

It was three o'clock in the afternoon and she was exhausted.

"Let's call it a day. You found shutters, you've gone for your walk, you've cried more tears than all the water from your two showers, and we've discovered an eternity of devotion. All in all, I'd say we've had an inordinate amount of success. Why don't you relax and take it easy?"

"You don't have to twist my arm for that one."

"What are you looking at?" He was behind her when she stood up.

"There are scratches in the corner. I was wondering where they came from."

"Oh, I can tell you that." His smile broadened as he caught her gaze. "I was nine, Freddy was six. Freddy tripped and splattered milk on the mirror and the glass turned cloudy. No one was around and I wanted to help because he wasn't supposed to come out of the kitchen or dining room with drinks or food. I ran to get steel wool to wipe the glass clean because that's what cook used when she spilled on the stove."

Laughter escaped as she imagined the nine-year-old William. "It was resourceful of you."

"I knew I was doing something wrong when my mother shouted my name." He went back to an obviously fond memory. "She stopped me before I had done too much damage, but she was never upset with me. She just showed me how to wet a rag and wipe it off properly."

"She sounds lovely."

"She was wonderful."

Love cocooned them as they watched each other in the glass. In his reflection, he was touching her. His hands smoothed over her hair that had grown past her shoulders and was curling at the ends. His head leaned forward as his arms circled her. He appeared to be kissing her neck. "I want you, Maisy. I shouldn't be able to feel such a need, but I do. I'm shocked at the desire you inflict."

Her head tilted back. He drew her and consumed her. "This could be an exercise in futility," she whispered. She opened her eyes, a sensual smile lurking.

"This is a path I can't go down with you," he said. His image disappeared.

A frown crossed her face as she tried to find him. "How did you do that?"

"Years of practice." His voice was warm, nearby, as he once again appeared in the mirror. "I'll tell you what. I was going to save this until you had a good night's sleep, but I want to show you something."

"I am content with what I have."

"I wish I was. My desire for you is startling. Let's go to your room."

Her head snapped to attention. "Seriously?"

"Yes." She loved how his changing expressions accentuated his dimples. "You have been a salvation." A grin played across his enticing lips. "But that's not why I'm asking you to meet me in the bedroom. If there was anything at all I could do about the attraction between us, trust me, we wouldn't be in the situation we're in. Come on."

She almost felt him. Everything about him made her heart race.

"I'm excited to show you this."

"And I'm excited to see whatever you have to show me. But honestly, there's nothing I need other than being able to kiss you."

He groaned. "Stop it, brat. Are you ready?"

"Sure," she said, following footsteps that were not even a whisper on the floor. "You hiding Fort Knox?"

"I don't know."

His words gave her pause.

She loved the sanctuary of her room. When she first arrived, she had chosen a soft gray for the walls to match the ocean on a cloudy morning. The window and door trim had been painted a bright, glossy white, and her bedspread was a soft lemon color with gray and white accents. The headboard and side tables were shiny black, and an oversized stuffed chair was the only other piece of furniture in her soothing haven. Her decorations were classic but simple, and she used the built-in dresser in the closet.

"My father concealed nooks in plain sight, like the firewood storage," he said. "Mother used to knit when we were here. The time here of not having to be anything but a wife and mother brought her peace, so she'd make us hats and scarves and mittens."

"I can't wait to see what condition they're in."

"After the Depression, my father was more cautious where he hid valuables, so when we built the cottage, he designed three nooks inside the house, in addition to the overhang for the shutters - the wood bin, the one I'm going to show you now, and one other."

"Good Lord."

"Yep. So I need you to close the door into this room. Then press on the left side of the left door frame."

She did as instructed and a long panel opened. There were guns, two fishing rods, and knit hats and gloves visible. There was also a small metal strongbox.

"Why don't you set what you find on the bed?" he asked. "I honestly don't know what's in there. He had a secret room at the big house and cubbyholes here, but I doubt he brought much more than he'd need for emergencies."

Maisy was as intrigued with the intricate intarsia

knitting as she was with the discovery of silver coins. There wasn't much, but their history was fascinating to her.

"You must have had such fun."

"It was a perfect life – until the War. My parents were loving and kind, my brother and I were always pals, or so I thought. And I had a woman I believed loved me as much as I loved her."

"Times were so different then, Wills. Women didn't have the freedom they do today. As horrid as Freddy ended up being, Mary Catherine was a victim of circumstance."

"That's kind of you to say."

"Think about the position she was in. Young, newly married, war breaks out, you find out you're pregnant but no one knows you're even married in a time when having a child out of wedlock was not acceptable in anyone's family, especially a family like yours. Then you believe your husband has been killed. It would be a nightmare. Today it would be okay to have the baby, but during the forties, her situation would have been a scandal."

"Thank you. In all of these years, I've never considered her condition in such a way. I never understood how she married him so quickly."

"What he did to you is unfathomable and unforgivable, but up until that time, he truly was upholding the family honor – even if he had been in love with her himself before then."

"I often wondered, but she and I were in love and I never thought of him as a threat."

"Lord willing, none of us would resort to murder, but Mary Catherine didn't know. You have to believe he never told her what he'd done. Even Freddy himself wasn't aware of what he was capable of until the end, so everything before then was horribly unfortunate but excusable."

"We were so young and innocent. We had no idea the realities of life outside our devoted and pampered existence. I doubt many were left unscathed by the War."

She set all of the items back the way they'd been found and secured the panel. "Thank you for showing me. I hope to never need anything in there, but it's good there are provisions in case of an emergency. And I'll find a gun expert and make sure the rifles are put in good working condition. Maybe Willie would like them."

"That thought pleases me."

"Finding these special places is exciting. They're treasures in and of themselves, and that you had a hand in their construction blows me away. And the shutters will be invaluable. Thank you."

"My pleasure. Who could have anticipated when we were building this place the needs and people who would come after us? But then, who could have imagined this unearthly existence?"

"Who indeed?" The events of the last twenty-four hours caught up with her and she was ready to collapse. "I'm going to call it a day if you don't mind."

"Not in the least. No more crying. Get a good night's sleep and let's start fresh in the morning."

"If I'm not up in eight hours, don't be concerned. My goal is to stay in bed until noon."

⚜ ELEVEN ⚜

August 1952

"Daddy, Daddy, come here."

"What is it, Willie?"

"There was a man in the mirror! He even knows my name!"

Freddy didn't have time for his son's foolishness. *"Why aren't you out playing with your brother?"*

"I came in to get water and saw someone. I've seen him before. He's really nice. He called me over and said, 'Hello, Willie.'"

"Get your drink and go back outside and stop bothering me."

"He told me to tell you that William sends his regards."

The glass dropped from Freddy's hand and the veins at his temples protruded. He grabbed his son's arm, jerking him around to face him. *"What did he look like?"*

The little boy tried to pull loose from his father's painful grip. *"Daddy, you're hurting me. Let go!"*

"What did he look like?" he shouted.

"He looked like the picture at the big house of grandpa. At first I thought Mama had brought it here."

Freddy straightened, color draining from his face. *"Did he say anything else?"* His voice was quiet.

Willie rubbed his arm. "He called me 'son' and said to tell you he'd see you around."

⁊ↄ⅃ↄ⅊

"**G**ood morning. You appear well rested."

"All that crying gave me a headache. Feels like I tied one on last night and now I'm paying the price with the morning-after hangover, but I'm motivated to do what needs to be done."

"Nothing a good cup of coffee won't cure. When you're finished writing, we can progress to the next phase, however that manifests itself."

"Oh, goodie."

"Sarcasm becomes you. Get your coffee."

"You're an authoritarian man, did you know that?"

"Ah, Maisy. That really isn't so. Not being able to do for you is frustrating. Were picking up an item within my power, your coffee would have been waiting with a pile of bacon, freshly baked toast, and your favorite over-easy eggs."

"Thank you. I love your consideration," she said, heading to the kitchen. "Sounds delicious, but the old juice of the java will have to suffice this morning."

"So what happens when you send off all of your story to Jonnell?"

"She's been reading what I've sent in parts, but generally when I'm finished she'll read the manuscript in its entirety for continuity, suggest edits, then when I get those done they do their magic."

"How long does their magic take?"

"Usually six to eight months from my final submission

until there's a published book."

"Hmmm . . ."

"What are you thinking?"

It took him a moment to answer. "You are a ray of light in my confused tunnel of darkness. But as much as you don't want to listen, you need a man of actual substance, not a shadow from the past who will never be able to be a partner to you, never be able to satisfy you. Hell, never be able to leave this house with you."

"Wills . . ."

"Don't. Let's finish the book and the future will take care of itself."

The following weeks were fun, intense, melancholy, exciting. Unlike anything she'd attempted before, hearing Wills' story gave flight to her imagination and grew their bond daily.

"You're doing this, you know," he said tenderly.

"Not sure what you mean."

"You're the one putting energy and life into what I'm telling you. I'm giving you facts, you're weaving the emotion. You truly have a gift."

"I'm ashamed to admit I spent so long hearing Josh tell me I'd never amount to much as a writer, that my stories were boring, so part of me believed what he said, even as I wanted desperately to prove him wrong."

"You're going to prove him wrong with this book, whether he's around to appreciate your talent or not."

"I hope you're right. I can't wait to deliver the finished work into the right hands, and if the story makes a splash, all the better." After a moment she asked, "Will you meet me in the study?"

"Of course."

A deep sigh escaped as her gaze embraced him.

"What is it?" He ran a thumb over her cheek, wishing she could feel him.

"There's a lot of magic my little machine can perform." Overwhelming love shone from her eyes. She typed a few words into her computer. "I found Willie."

"You . . . How? Where?" He stood behind her.

"Are you ready to know about him?"

"Maisy . . ."

"Ready?"

"Of course."

"Willie became a lawyer for the family business. He's retired now, is seventy-four years old, lives with his wife, Betty, in Kennebunkport in the summer and has a home in Sarasota, Florida, where they spend their winters when they're not travelling. They have three children – twin boys, Jonathan and Donovan, whom I believe you saw when they were young and when Donovan owned this house, and a daughter named Mary. Being the first girl in the family in generations, Mary was spoiled by her father and her brothers."

"How did you find all this out?"

"There's this amazing tool called Google," she said.

"And it found them?"

She shrugged. "It gave me the information I needed."

"There are no words . . ."

"I was thrilled. I didn't spend time with the man I bought this place from. The attorneys handled the details and I didn't even meet him. I didn't want to make anyone's acquaintance because I was running away and didn't want emotional attachments, but he was your grandson! And Jonathan and Sarah? He was also your grandson! I would have done things so differently had I understood the implications then."

"We can only use the information we have at any point in time. Don't beat yourself up for what you didn't know."

"Were you aware of who he was when he was living here?"

"Yes, but he wasn't here much. He looked like Freddy, and he'd bring different girls here but never stayed long. There was nowhere for me to escape to get away at times." He laughed at the memory. "Some days I would literally sing out loud to drown out noises because no one could hear me if I didn't want them to."

"That must have been uncomfortable! Grandsons bringing paramours here, despondent young widows crying at least five hours a day."

"It was never awkward with you, you have to believe me. Long before you knew of my presence, I thought of you as 'my Maisy.' You captivated me, but all I wanted was to ease your sorrow. I was so afraid you'd leave me, and I loved having you here . . . regardless of how much noise you were making."

She gasped. They both laughed.

"Are you ready to see him, Wills? Are you ready to see your son?"

"What do you mean?"

"I have lots of photos of him and his children. He was a popular personality and then married a socialite, so there are hundreds of photographs through the years."

He seemed lost. "I've waited so long."

"Then let's get this party started," she teased. The earliest photo appeared on her screen. She had gone to great lengths to arrange the file in chronological order so Wills saw the progression as Willie aged. She was watching the mirror as his eyes were riveted to the pictures on the computer, his mouth agape.

"He looks like me!"

"Of course he does. He's your son."

"But exactly like me."

"Yes, I must admit I was taken aback initially as I started doing research."

"You can't know . . ."

"No, I have no concept," she said sympathetically.

They shared their feelings through their expressions. "If I had nothing else, this would be enough."

Her heart ached for what he'd suffered and what he'd lost. "I had such pleasure being able to do this for you."

"Please continue."

They sat for over an hour going through the slideshow Maisy had put together. "To say I'm overwhelmed is an understatement. Seeing Willie grow up, get married, have children . . . from the bottom of my heart, thank you."

"Don't thank me. It was all Google. I just know how to search to my advantage."

"I don't understand, but I don't need to."

"No, you don't need to."

"You must be exhausted. Let's call it a day. Grab yourself a glass of wine if you want and we can talk in front of the fire."

"Sounds divine. I'll meet you there."

"We're almost done with the story, Maisy."

Lying in the dark on the couch, the glow from the flames illuminating the room, she was in a playful mood.

"That pre-supposes I'm going to finish."

"Can you imagine how Jonnell would react if you told her now, with only a few chapters left, that you've decided you're giving up?"

"I shudder to think. It would be a nightmare of epic proportions."

"To say nothing of the fact that we would only be delaying the inevitable."

Her mood turned thoughtful. "What's going to happen, Wills?"

"You're going to finish your bestselling novel, meet your complete man, and live happily ever after."

"Stop it. I'm serious."

"So am I, Maisy. I see great victories for you."

"How long will you stay?"

"Even I don't know the answer, any more than I understand how I know this is what I need to do to be released. I'll be here as long as necessary."

She didn't want him to see her tears.

"You must trust you're going to be okay."

"I can't bear the thought of you being gone," she said, her voice catching.

"You survived in this setting for years before you knew about me. You grew stronger daily. You can do whatever you set your mind to. You're tough."

"But now that I found you . . ."

"Let's talk about what happens with the book. You send the finished manuscript off to Jonnell. Then what?"

"I do my edits, we go back and forth until they tell me they don't need me anymore, then we wait."

"Six months?"

"Usually."

"Can you print up the story before the actual book comes out?"

"Sure, I can make a copy and have it bound."

"Would you mind doing that?"

"Not at all."

"Then I would be obliged if you would deliver the bound document directly to Willie."

She didn't know what to say.

"Is that possible?"

"I don't see why not. I can track him down, but I'm not sure how I'll convince him I'm not a lunatic."

"I have been thinking about that very situation, and I'm pretty sure I have a way to convince him you're telling the truth. With your permission, I'd like to show you something in your bedroom."

"I thought you'd never ask," she teased. "Come on."

"This was my parent's room. My mother didn't bring jewelry with her when they came to the cottage, but this was another secret place my father built for fun. This one was for my mother's personal belongings, but I had need of its ease and secrecy once, as you'll see."

Maisy was used to his voice next to her, but she hated not being able to watch him when they spoke. "Children through the years played Cowboys and Indians here. There should be a headdress hidden."

"Show me!"

She almost heard him smile. "The casing under the window sill . . . push on the right side. Push hard and quick."

The wood underneath popped out a few inches. "Oh, look!"

She pulled gently to open the molding to a forty-five degree angle, exposing a long, narrow inset. "Wills, this is brilliant!"

"Thank you, ma'am. Again, I wish I could take the credit but the inventiveness was my father's. Do you see any feathers?"

"Yes!" she said, removing them reverently. "And the beading is intricate. Wills! Your initials are on it!"

"My mother beaded it for me when I was a child. She often said sitting in a rocking chair and doing the handcrafts of yesteryears was the only truly relaxing pastime she had. After we built the cottage, she brought many of her earlier crafts and decorated with them."

Maisy peered inside the opening. "Did you know there was a letter in here?"

"No! Would you please retrieve it?"

She took the sepia colored envelope out of its hiding place. "It's still sealed. Who do you suppose it's from?"

"My mother."

She turned toward his voice behind her shoulder. "How do you know that?"

"I recognize her handwriting." His voice was reverent and gentle.

"It's addressed to you."

"Would you mind very much getting a letter opener and slitting the top gently? She obviously put it in there decades ago."

She sat on the edge of the bed. "Do you want to read it?"

"I'm happy to have you do so. Since I can't hold it, you will have to do the honors."

Her voice was anguished as she recited the long-dormant contents.

My darling William. You and I are the only ones alive who know of this special place. If you never return, this letter will remain as long as the house stands. Nothing in me believes you are dead. They brought word months ago that you had been killed in Algeria but your body has not been found.

Don't you think a mother would know if her son was gone? I pray for you constantly, knowing in my heart you are still alive but having no idea how to find you. I would move heaven and earth to see your beloved face again. I have contacted every diplomat in our acquaintance to have them investigate your whereabouts.

Even the recent birth of my grandson who bears your name cannot dull the pain of your loss. Until they return your body, I will not accept your death, nor will this mother's heart stop searching for you.

Nothing about this seems right. You and Mary Catherine were so devoted to each other. How can she and Freddy be married and be parents so soon? And your father . . . he gave up his will to live when they told us you had been killed. I'm so alone but have not given up hope.

Along with this letter, you will find my mother's ring that I wore every day of your life. It will not grace my hand again until you walk through these doors.

I love you, William Andrew, and will until the day they lay me to rest . . . Mother.

Maisy sat on the edge of the bed. "Oh, Wills." Her heart broke for the lives that had been shattered by senseless tragedies. "I'm so sorry." She felt lost. "I want to take you in my arms and hold you. I want to give you comfort and mourn with you for all that was lost."

There was no response. "Wills?"

She crossed to the board that stood perpendicular to the wall and reached further inside. Her fingers found a small, cold object. She withdrew an intricate sapphire ring. "Do you recognize this?"

After a moment, his hoarse voice whispered, "It belonged to my mother."

She opened her hand in the direction of his voice. "It's exquisite."

"It was one of her favorite possessions. My father used to tell her the color reminded him of her eyes. All of my life she told me the ring would pass to my bride when I grew up because my eyes were the same intensity as hers."

She stood silently, almost able to see his memories with him. "What do you want me to do with them?" she asked.

"If you don't mind, I'd like you to set the letter and ring on your desk in the study so I can view them at leisure. And would you put the headdress back, please? When the time comes, I know exactly how it shall be used."

She put the little boy's crown in place just as she'd found it and closed the cover. If she hadn't opened the casing herself, she would never have believed its existence.

"So you had her eye color?"

"Yes, I looked like my father, but my eyes were identical to hers. She told me often she saw herself staring back from my face. When I was very young her words didn't mean much. As I grew older, the similarity was a secret we shared, like she had given me a special part of herself."

She set the ring in a crystal bowl on her desk and propped the letter open. When their eyes met in the mirror, his smile was poignant. "It's time to finish the book, Maisy. I need my son to know who his father was."

~~~ TWELVE ~~~

July 1953

"Hello, Freddy."

Freddy spun around like a thief, breath quickening, hair standing on end. There was no one there. Many times he thought he was on the verge of insanity, cloaking himself with a fragile façade of normalcy. He often thought he heard William, once he even thought he saw him. He went to the kitchen to pour himself another drink.

"Didn't expect to see me again?"

The voice sounded like William, but why did he laugh?

"Who are you?" Freddy backed against the wall as he went to the living room. "Identify yourself!"

"Oh, Freddy, you're aware of who I am. I mean, in truth, you only had one brother, correct? One brother whom you loved very much. One brother you pledged to honor and protect. But then something happened, didn't it, Freddy? Greed got in the way. You decided the better part of valor would be to . . ."

"Shut up! Do you hear me? Shut up!"

"Tsk. Tsk. So much anger from such a loving sibling."

"Where are you?"

"Right here in the room with you. Watching your every

move."

Freddy had to quit drinking. He had well and truly lost his mind. He stood in front of his mother's treasured mirror and looked at his bloodshot eyes and noticed how unkempt he appeared. Mary Catherine had been asking him to see a doctor. Maybe she was right. He was rapidly losing his grip on reality. He stepped closer to see the grey hairs he had grown when he caught a movement behind him.

He turned quickly, knocking a fountain pen off the table. The room was empty. He turned back to his reflection.

"Cat got your tongue, Freddy?"

"William?" He whispered the word, afraid on so many levels.

"Yours truly, little brother."

"What are you doing here?" His head hurt from the confusion. Was that really William in the mirror, actually speaking?

"Where else would I want to be than with my devoted family? Remember all those times you and I stood in front of this very mirror, talking about growing up, talking about how we'd always take care of one another?"

"You have to believe me, William, I didn't know what else to do. I thought about it for days and no other solution presented itself. I've grieved since the day you died but I couldn't undo what had been done."

"Yes, I've seen how sorry you've been. Loving my wife, abusing my son."

"No! I love him! He's my son!"

"You have a strange way of showing it. I've watched you take your wrath out on him while James was left unscathed."

"What do you want? Why are you here?"

"It's too late for me, but I will hunt you down and you will suffer the same fate as I, only much more slowly and painfully, if *you ever so much as lay another hand on my son. His pain is my pain. Don't think for a minute I won't be watching you. Do I make myself perfectly clear?"*

"I swear. Never again. You have my word."

"Yes, we're both acquainted with how well you honor your word."

⟨⌒⟩⌒⟩

The last chapter was sent by the end of the month. The next phase would soon begin. "I'm afraid, Wills."

"Of what, dearest?"

"Of a future I'm unsure of."

"But isn't that what life is, really? Which one of us can be privy to what lies in wait for us tomorrow? There's so much we would change were we able. But it's not for us to have such knowledge, and you will face whatever happens bravely, regardless of what those circumstances are."

After several minutes she asked, "Where will you go?"

"I can't see past this junction either, Maisy. Don't ask me how, but what I do know is my family needed the truth for me to be released, but I don't have a grasp of what form that freedom will take."

"Are you afraid?"

"No, except for the loss of you, I'm ready."

"Will you promise me something?"

"I would deny you nothing in my power to provide."

"Will you promise to make an attempt to contact me somehow, someway? I'm not sure I can survive thinking one day you'll just be gone and there's no hope of ever communicating with you again."

"You're irrepressible. You'll do admirably."

"I am what I've become because of your faith in me. I was a mess when I got here." Her voice caught, but she refused to dissolve into sorrow.

"You have the recollection all wrong. You spent every day getting tougher mentally and physically. I didn't do anything for you, only helped you recognize what you had done for yourself."

"What if I can't finish?"

"Maisy, would you let me down when we've come this far? Would we have gone through all of this only for you to throw in the towel now? Of course not."

"Of course not," she said faintly. "But you're giving me more credit than I deserve."

"Never. One day you'll realize your worth."

The waning October days were getting colder, the nights advancing earlier. "When did your family normally secure the shutters?"

"We didn't stay this late in the season. We would put them on early in September so we'd be home in time for classes, and wouldn't return until spring or early summer."

"The weather's still mild. I can wait to put them up."

"Have you heard from Jonnell?"

She didn't answer as she wandered into the study.

"Maisy?"

"Yes, I heard from her on Monday."

"Why didn't you tell me?"

"Because I've been trying to figure out what I wanted to do. Because I'm not ready to face the end of the book yet. Because, quite frankly, I didn't want to."

"I understand," he said softly. "What did she say?"

"That it was one of the best stories she'd read in years.

That she can't wait for it to be published. That it's going to put me on the map and they want to offer me a three-book deal."

"That's great news!"

"Great news? *Great news?*" She addressed the man standing at her shoulder. "Does no one understand what my perceived brilliance is going to cost me?"

"Listen to me. Stop beating yourself up." His hands caressed her shoulders, her arms. "When will you trust you did this? My story had intrigue, but you're the one who made the words come to life. You *are* brilliant. Recognize your ability."

"I'm a fraud. How can I possibly write more without my muse?"

She welcomed his arms as they wrapped around her, his lips as they trailed up her neck. "Think of me and this moment when you hit the *New York Times* Bestseller list with each successive book, and don't ever forget *you* accomplished this. You, Margaret Marie Hollis, are the one who had the talent all along. I just helped you discover the words trapped in your soul."

"When you first knew me I cried all the time. I fear I will end our relationship with perpetual tears."

"Only for a while, my love," he said softly. "You're not the same woman who showed up here that fateful summer." He was beside her, his fingers trailing across her cheek. "You'll see. Now I want to tell you how I think we should best approach Willie."

"Good, because short of having him come to Summerset, I have no idea how to convince him."

"I don't know how I know, but meeting him is not possible. He needs to hear the truth but he doesn't need to see me. My time here is limited, so I have a plan to make him believe you."

"I enjoy our time on the couch in front of the fire. I can't see you but I'm aware you're there beside me. Let's settle in and you can weave your ideas into reality."

The flames licked the chimney and it was comfortable and warm. "I'm not sure I'll ever be able to thank you for preparing the wood and the starter bags for me. The solace of the fireplace is to me what your mother's handiwork was to her."

"I was a much more patient person than Freddy, but I must admit I got bored making dozens of those sacks and carrying in a cord of firewood. Knowing how much they benefit you, it makes the effort all worthwhile."

"I love almost everything about you, Wills. I love your heart and your mind and your stunning face and your encouragement and your ability to make me feel again."

"*Almost* everything?"

"I don't love your invisible quality." She laughed, but she wasn't really kidding. "I want to touch you all the time. I want to kiss you and make love to you. I want to lie in your arms and have you tell me these stories. And I don't ever want you to leave."

"Don't do this to us, sweetheart. I would do anything for you, but I can't change this. So let me tell you this story. It appears to be a faultless solution."

"So what do you think, Maisy? Do you think a headband with his initials that I helped him hide almost seventy years ago will jog his memory enough to believe you?"

"Did you see inside when he put it there?"

"No. I stood in the doorway making sure no one was coming. Why?"

"I keep thinking your mother's letter would already have been there. He wouldn't have been tall enough to see, and if you weren't actually peering into the darkness, you wouldn't have seen whatever was there either."

"One thing I've learned on this journey is, everything happens in its own time. I found the letter when I was supposed to find the letter. Now you can take the ring and one of the photos with it on my mother's hand, and the headdress. That should be enough to convince him what you're telling him is the truth."

"Okay, I'll find out where he is and arrange a meeting."

"How will you do that?"

"Technology, Wills, technology."

⚜

"Yes, Mr. Raines. I promise I won't take much of your time, but the information about your family is vital. Yes, of course. I'll see you Saturday at noon. Can you verify the address? I'll see you then. Thank you, sir."

"What did he say?"

"They're not leaving for Sarasota until after Christmas this year and he'll meet me in two days at his home."

"It was my home."

"*What?*"

"You wrote down the address. He must have inherited the family home. That pleases me more than you can imagine. Let's rehearse what you're going to say so you go in assertive. I'll tell you about the layout of the house, I'll tell you about the people in the photos, where my mother's mirror used to hang. I'll even tell you about my father's secret room. No one else is even aware of its existence now. And you'll have the beaded headband. He'll have to believe you."

"You may not fret about this, do you understand? Do you think I'd let you come this far and not convince him before I come home? It'll be like eggs in the coffee."

His laughter brought her joy. "Do people still use that expression? I'm sure they don't, but I welcome the encouragement that it will be easy."

"He'll believe me or I'll die trying."

"Don't tease, but I do appreciate your assurance. Do you have the manuscript?"

"Yes. I printed it last night. I'll bind it today and that part of it will be out of the way."

"What if all of our planning doesn't work?" he asked.

"Now which one of us is lacking confidence? You have to trust me. I won't give up until your goal has been accomplished."

"I know. It's just that . . ."

"Tell me what's going on?"

"I'm actually not sure. I've waited seventy years for this and I'm reacting like a swain on his first date."

"You have nothing to worry about. The meeting will turn out fine, you'll see."

"Maisy."

"Yes?"

"I can't see the future. I'm not sure what's on the other side. But whatever happens, however our circumstance ends up, I want you to always remember . . . you're the best thing that ever happened to me."

She tried to catch the sob as it escaped. "Don't, please. I have to be strong. I can't fall apart like a dying rose until this is over."

"You're not going to fall apart. Grab the photos and I'll

tell you who everyone is."

They spent their remaining time going over information only Wills would have been privy to, Maisy learning family secrets that Willie might be aware of but few other living souls would.

"Promise me you'll be here when I get back. Promise."

"I can't promise what I don't know, but if it's at all within my power, I'll be waiting right here when you walk back through the door."

"Wills . . ."

"Me too, Maisy. Now go. The sooner you leave, the sooner you'll be back."

⸎

She was sure her heart would explode as she waited at the massive entrance to the mansion that had been Wills' home. A maid opened the front door and escorted her silently into an impressive library, the appearance of which she knew before she entered. Stepping into the room, a gasp escaped and her hand flew to her chest as she came face to face with a life-sized portrait of Wills.

The man she had been profoundly acquainted with all these months was a pale reflection of the magnificence of the vision before her. Anguish burst unheeded as she saw what was much more of a lifelike version of the man she loved.

"Many people react similarly when they see that photo of my uncle," said the compassionate voice behind her. She turned to greet him. "He was a dynamic man," he continued. "Died way too soon."

Again she was stunned by the flesh and blood translation standing before her, albeit almost fifty years older than the William she knew.

"Willie?" she asked in a whisper, emotion choking her at a time when she needed her wits and composure.

His booming laugh caught her off guard. "I was charmed by your beauty when you walked in, but I haven't been called Willie since I was ten years old."

"I'm Margaret," she said, taking his extended hand in both of hers. She couldn't take her eyes off him.

"We're going to get along famously," he teased. "Anyone who has the nerve to call me Willie must have a lot of spunk. Please, have a seat." He closed the door behind him and motioned for her to sit in a plush leather chair as he sat in one opposite her.

"Is that Freddy?" She nodded toward the portrait hanging beside her beloved.

"You couldn't possibly have known my father." His head tilted, voice rising slightly.

"He wasn't . . ." *No, that wasn't the way to begin this conversation,* she thought. "If you have a little time to spare, I have a fascinating story to tell you."

"All the time in the world, young lady. I'm listening."

They were secluded in a world of rare books, talking secretively, sharing stories. She started slowly, but by the time she pulled out the headdress from his childhood, he not only believed her, but they had become fast friends. They took short breaks throughout the day, had a meal delivered to their inner sanctum, then talked late into the night.

She had explained parts of the story to him, but when she gave him the manuscript, she slipped quietly from the room so he could read in private. Betty invited Maisy to join her in an enclosed terrace overlooking the well-manicured lawns that were ablaze with light. Their time was relaxing as they became acquainted, although Maisy revealed few of the details of her visit, leaving that task to whatever Willie wanted to share with his charming wife.

Willie had made arrangements for her to stay in the room that belonged to Wills most of his life. She could almost feel the young man he had been as she closed her eyes and fell exhausted into bed in the middle of the night, into a sleep full of sepia-colored dreams.

They all woke late the next morning and enjoyed a leisurely brunch. Willie and Maisy excused themselves and continued their exchange. Before she returned home she showed him the hiding place in his master bedroom closet. She was pleased with his shock and excitement at the discovery of a room that had remained a secret for decades.

They walked through the manor house, Maisy sharing stories of events that happened in each room that no one else could have known. He asked questions, she answered as best she could. What she didn't know, she promised to find out.

Betty and Willie stood with her as she was leaving. "Don't be a stranger," he said, taking her in a warm embrace. "You've given me a new life."

"This could have had such a different outcome. Thank you for listening to me."

Betty looked at her husband and the young girl standing in the open doorway, questions evident in her eyes. Willie brought her hand to his lips, turning toward Maisy. "My wife knows me as a sane and rational man," he said, smiling. "I'm not sure how I will convince her I haven't stepped off the deep end."

"Maybe start with a book and take if from there," she

said. Her car was waiting in the circular drive, and she waved as she got inside. She couldn't wait to get home.

ᒷᑖᒲᑋᒣᑫ

The two days she was gone felt as long as the previous seventy-five years to him. He was weak with relief when the key turned in the lock.

"My God, Maisy, I thought you'd never come back."

"Oh, Wills, it was all you wanted and more," she said, excitement evident as she set her suitcase down and locked the door behind her. "I didn't want to leave there, but I was so anxious . . ."

She stood, arms at her sides, mouth open, astonished.

"What is it? What's the matter?" His voice was raised as he approached her.

Her voice was a whisper. "I can see you."

He put his hands on her shoulders. "What do you mean?" he asked, turning to find where the mirror was in relation to where they stood.

Her eyes focused on him like a magnifying glass targeting a pinpoint of light into flame. "Wills, I can see you. Standing in front of me, touching me, looking around." Her expression alternated between joy and shock.

"Can you feel me?" he asked, running his knuckles down her cheek.

Her eyes closed, savoring this new awareness. "No, but I can see what you're doing."

"Not with your eyes closed you can't," he teased.

Her eyes flew open and she leaned her head back to study every inch of his face. "Why didn't I realize before how tall you were?"

"Because you've never been able to see me when we were face to face. But I wasn't so tall. Not over six feet. I suppose most people would seem to tower over your small frame." He couldn't stop touching her.

"Why can I see you now?" she asked, treasuring the vision.

"I have no idea. Maybe it's the intense emotion you're feeling, we're feeling – enough to generate a sensory bond between us."

"Okay, I can wrap my brain around that possibility. I loved you so much while I was there, knowing I was in the home you grew up in, loving Willie as he listened enthralled to stories you shared that no one else knew."

"You've been on emotional overload for so long, but this is a condition I never anticipated."

"The entire drive home I was anxious to walk through the door and share with you, to tell you how exciting my visit was and how perfectly the scenes played out. If we had choreographed the events before I left, nothing we could have planned would have made our meeting go better than it did."

"So he believed you?"

"He not only believed me, he cried because he was so thankful."

"Sit down. Tell me. Do you want some wine? A fire? I didn't know when you'd be back, but it's not like I had the ability to prepare for your arrival even if I had known." His tone was pleasant but mocking.

"Enough. What we have is so much more than enough. I can't believe this," she said, touching the outline of his face as he sat on the couch next to her. "Dear God, you're irresistibly beautiful."

His tenderness warmed her heart. "Likewise. More

than once you're attraction has stopped me in my tracks when I've looked at you."

"Really?" she said, finding an odd sort of healing in his words. "I think I wanted to see you so much that we somehow made your spirit visible. Soon I'll be able to actually feel you, but for now, I'm so grateful."

"That would be a miracle. And what did you mean, 'he cried'?"

"He's carried guilt for most of his life because he hated Freddy. Even as he grew a little older and Freddy became marginally kinder, Willie couldn't shake the notion he didn't belong, that something wasn't right."

"Smart kid."

"Indeed. A sense of detachment often happens when children have been adopted but aren't aware of the circumstances of their birth, they just never adapt to the new family. Many times they consider themselves the odd man out. That's how Willie felt. He said he and his brother James talked about his isolation occasionally, but James never understood what he meant."

"Was he nice to you?"

"From the moment I stepped through the front door, we were like old friends. That may have been because I had such a familiarity with him, and as soon as I got past my nervousness, I knew he was near and dear to my heart. I knew him so well, knew things about him even he didn't know."

"Were you awkward at first?"

"Funny you should ask. What made me most self-conscious during my visit was my awareness of him as your son. I relate to you as a man in his late twenties. Willie is in his seventies. He's still relatively young, but I kept trying to envision you as his father, and even for my animated imagination, putting that into a neat package was a stretch."

"A sensory time warp, I'm sure. How did you convince him?"

"There was no going back when I gave him the beaded headdress. When I repeated your words about the initials, he was a believer. He hugged me and cried as though we were family and had known each other all our lives. Then he took the manuscript and read the dedication and he was my devoted servant," she said teasingly.

"I loved the simplicity of it," Wills said. *"This book is dedicated to William Andrew Raines. The beginning. The middle. The end.* What did he do then?"

"He stayed up reading while Betty and I got acquainted."

"It sounds like your stay was all we could have hoped for."

"I'm overwhelmingly pleased. I took lots of photos of him and the homestead. Do you want me to show you?"

"Maybe tomorrow. You've had a busy few days. Why don't you unpack and call it a night?"

"Because you're here. Because you're visible. Do you think sleep would make up for the excitement of this breakthrough?"

His expression was gentle and sad as he touched her face. "I've missed you."

"I want to feel your warm, translucent hands on me. Seeing you touch me has my flesh weeping with desire, but it's not quite satisfying."

He leaned forward, his lips appearing to come in contact with her upturned face.

Her breath quickened. "I want you, Wills."

"I know. I know." He wrapped her in his arms. "Thank

you. So many dreams fulfilled in our acquaintance. And for the gift of my son, I will be indebted for eternity."

"He wanted to come back with me, did I tell you that?"

"No! What did you say?"

"I told him such an introduction wasn't possible now, but that maybe sometime down the road he'd be able to visit."

Wills didn't respond at first, but his smile was thoughtful. "He won't recognize this place," he said, finally. "You've made every corner bright and cheerful. When we built it, the idea was rustic. You've made Summerset a home."

His thumb continued to stroke her cheek.

"Now that the book's done and I look back on our journey," she said, "I feel like a fugitive from some conjured fantasy. Rod Serling had nothing on us."

The red rays of the retreating sun shone across the living room, making his form radiant. "I'm glad you made it home before the first snowfall."

~ THIRTEEN ~

July 1953

"What happened to your mother's mirror?" Mary Catherine asked her husband as he crammed clothes into his suitcase.

"Roger Schierholz came over with his boys to see if Willie and James wanted to play with them. He kept admiring the mirror, so I told him to take it."

"Why would you do that? It was her favorite possession."

"She doesn't come here anymore, and opening up the cottage all the time is too much trouble. I'm planning on curtailing our visits. Schierholz loved the mirror, was pleased to get it, and someone should enjoy it if we're not going to be here."

"We should have taken it home, Freddy."

He thought of the vision of William and shuddered. He never wanted to see that ghastly mirror again. He had thought seriously of breaking it, but Roger knocked before he had time to accomplish the deed. Good riddance.

"The mirror should have gone to our boys. You know how much your mother treasured it."

"Yes, and she's dead and the mirror's not here. Drop it. Get the boys and pack up. We're leaving today."

"But why? They'll be disappointed to go back so soon."

"*I won't stay another day. Get our things together. We're going.*"

"*But Freddy . . .*"

"*Don't argue with me, Mary Catherine. We'll be home before dark, but I don't ever want to spend another night in this place.*"

⸎

"*I* have to meet Jonnell in Augusta in two days. Then I'll pop in for a quick visit with my folks and be back before the sun sets."

"Is she pleased?"

"Sure seems to be."

"I'm thrilled for you. Sounds like you're going to get your big break."

"We almost have it all now, don't we?"

"What do you mean?"

"You gave me this remarkable novel, we have each other, we have this sanctuary we both love, and I can actually *see* you!"

"You're the one who gave life to *The Conflict of Wills*. I'll accept the role of muse for this one, but you've always had the ability in you."

"When I come home in a few days, we'll have to talk about the next book. Do we start fresh with a completely different angle, or do we take one of the characters from the first story and do a spin off?"

"Yes."

"Thanks. You're a lot of help this evening."

"Get some rest."

"Wills?"

"Yes?"

"I have a favor to ask."

"If it's in my power."

"I know our restrictions, but would you at least lie down with me while I fall asleep?"

He groaned. "That's not a good idea, Maisy."

"It's not like I can touch you. I just want you there, for us to be together."

"I can never find a way to say 'no' to you. Go get ready for bed. I'll join you shortly."

Her grin told him she considered that a victory.

He gave her time to settle before he joined her. The darkness was heavy and there was no movement of the bed as he lay down beside her.

"Where have you been?"

"How did you know I was here?"

"You're kidding, right? You may not be touchable, but I feel your presence everywhere. Even when we're not in the same room I know where you are."

"Is it a sense?"

"I have no idea," she said, yawning. "Even if I can't see you, I can still – perceive you, for lack of a better word."

When she was soundly asleep, his spirit was restless. He wandered the four walls, less driven but more lost than he'd been since arriving. Something was happening he didn't understand but he wasn't sure he had ever truly comprehended the depths of his abilities or his limitations, and he was prepared for whatever was to come next.

There was a new awareness of her the next morning. He felt as though he was almost mortal, and their minds blended in a way previously unknown to them. The sensations were new, strange, not unpleasant but different than what they'd had before. She was as conscious of the change as he.

"You're so real to me I can almost touch you."

"Changes are happening. I'm trying to pinpoint what is altered, but I, too, have a keener sense of you."

"That's exciting," she said, going into the study. "Wills?"

"Yes, I believe you should."

"I should what?" she asked, puzzled.

"You've been thinking of helping Traci's son, haven't you?"

"How did you . . ."

"I have no idea how," he said. "But I've seen you debating the pros and cons. If Josh was alive, he would be paying to support his child, correct? Is that the sense I've picked up from you?"

Astonished, she nodded.

"And despite how you were betrayed, Traci has been a good mother to young Josh."

"How could you possibly know that?"

"I'm only aware of what I'm sensing from you. I have no concept how I'm recognizing your thoughts because this is totally new to me, and right now I'm trying to verify with you what my senses are telling me."

"You're exactly right. Traci is struggling financially and Josh left a considerable amount of money. I'm not hurting, but I'm not sure how to proceed."

"For you to do what you're thinking of doing, you still don't have to have a relationship with her if that's not your desire. I sense that as your biggest hesitation."

"It is."

"You don't even have to speak to her. Set up a trust, a savings account, whatever is judicious. You can put in a lump sum or feed money monthly. Someone else can notify her of its existence. There would be nothing unreasonable for him to have taken care of his son, and your generosity of spirit is not out of line to provide for his child, regardless of the circumstances of his birth. And you are financially able."

The air vibrated like the humming strings of a harp as they watched each other. "I'm comfortable with what you're suggesting," she said, "and you've solved my concern of involvement. I do *not* desire to renew my relationship with her, nor do I want to share in his upbringing, but I do want to make sure he is being provided for."

He nodded in agreement.

"What I am more interested in at this moment is how this is happening," she said quietly.

"We don't need to understand. We've obviously reached a higher plane of interaction, but I have no idea how or why."

"Well I, for one, am loving this deeper dimension that goes along with being able to see you. And I appreciate your insight and input. When I'm in Augusta tomorrow, I'll stop by the bank and set up an account."

"That's just one of the reasons I love you," he said.

"Which one of the dozens are you referring to?" she teased.

"Because I don't know many people who would support their spouse's bastard child willingly, and yet you nurtured the idea to maturity in your heart with no one else's suggestion. You're an admirable person, Maisy Hollis."

She lowered her head to hide the blush. "I'm not doing anything anyone else wouldn't do under similar circumstances."

"That's not true. You are a gem sparkling more brightly than all the others."

"You'll give me a big head."

"I loved you at your darkest. When you thought there was no reason to go on, you picked yourself up day after day when you didn't want to. Your limp is almost non-existent, due solely to your perseverance. You've written a brilliant book that is going to set you apart.

"And now when you cry, it's usually from tenderness and your kind heart because you've learned how to face your demons and rise above the bitterness that so easily might have swallowed you. My love for you is boundless."

Sorrow tightened her chest. She wanted desperately to feel his lips as they touched her forehead, his thumb as it stroked her cheek, his arms as they wrapped around her.

"I want you to enjoy those sensations too." He turned and walked away. "Now let's get you ready for your meeting with Jonnell tomorrow. Is there a specific purpose?"

"She said she has exciting news for me and I want to pitch her a few scenarios I have for a new book."

"That's my girl." His look was compassionate. "Do you have any desire to finish your first story?"

"I'm more ready now than I was, and I might even explain to her why I was unable to write it before, but I have some other concepts I've been kicking around that I want to run by her."

"I'm pleased with how your creative juices are flowing. Every one of your ideas will make for an exciting book. You won't have a problem fulfilling a three-book deal."

Her laugh was immediate and came from her soul. "Dear Lord, I'm going to have to control my thoughts . . . or maybe not. When you can see what I imagine we can do when we're lying naked in each other's arms, our time might prove even more interesting."

His was groaning amusement. "You wouldn't conceive of the notion that a form without human anatomy could ache like this. I'm here to confirm that theory is wrong."

"There probably aren't a lot of theories on the subject, my love, but since we've progressed to a point of me not needing a mirror to see you, when I come back, I think we should take a few days and discover how far we can develop the tactile sensitivities of our relationship."

"While I fear we might find ourselves in a test of futility, I am, of course, willing to experiment with any possibility to bring you pleasure."

The new awareness between them was almost tangible and had them casting knowing glances and sly nuances at each other that hadn't existed before.

"Okay, it's eight o'clock," Maisy said as she was preparing to leave the following morning. "I'll be to the bank in Augusta by ten, should have my business completed by eleven, will stop and visit my folks, then I'm meeting Jonnell at one thirty. Realistically she and I will be together for a few hours, so I'll be home by seven at the absolute latest."

"I've been alone for decades, but the thought of you not being here for even half a day is enough to send me to my imaginary knees." He was stroking her cheek. She leaned in to his touch.

"Yes, keep that vision alive. I'm willing to work on the next phase when you return."

"I'll be as quick as I can, I promise."

When his lips touched hers, a gentle electric current flowed through her. "Did you feel that?" she asked with excitement. Her eyes were watching him intently, pulse pounding, breath quickening.

"I'm not sure if it was coming from me or you, but I'm willing to explore all of the avenues of this new relationship."

"Wills . . ."

"You need to go now. A storm is imminent, and even for more than selfish reasons it will be good if you're home before dark."

"Yes, master. You're still bossing me around."

"Don't give me your sass. None of it would matter if I didn't love you as much as I do."

"I know," she said as she slung her bag over her shoulder and headed for the garage. "Leave the lights on," she teased.

"Flipping switches is not a part of my current abilities, ma'am. Leave them on yourself."

The door shut on her laughter, then immediately opened again. "Hey, Wills?" she said, peering around the corner.

"Yes?"

"You flip *my* switches. I love you."

All of the emotion in his soul was staring back at her. "I know you do, Maisy. And you do it very well."

Her smile lit the room like fireworks in a dark sky.

The day had been more of a success than expected and she and Jonnell were finishing their meal. "Whatever change has transformed you, I'm thrilled. You look better than I've ever seen you, I love your longer hair, and your face is positively glowing."

"Yeah, Castine has been good for me." She leaned her cheek on her hand, thinking of how Wills had touched her there this morning. "Summerset was a godsend, and I don't think I've ever been this happy in my life."

"Is a man involved? Come on, we're old friends, you can tell me."

Maisy's smile was secretive. "Not really. I'm learning how to survive and am getting comfortable with my own company."

"So I'm loving all three of your ideas," Jonnell said. "Which one has you the most excited right now?"

"Probably the one about the New York lawyer inheriting the Bed and Breakfast in an obscure Western town. I think I can make . . ."

"Then that's the one you should start with. What are you thinking as far as . . . what's the matter? What happened? You look like you've seen a ghost!"

Maisy jumped up from her chair and grabbed her purse. "I'm sorry, Jonnell. Something awful is going on. I have to go! I'll call you in a few days."

"Wait a minute. How do you know? You were in the middle of a sentence."

"I just know. I'll call you," she said, rushing to her car, hoping beyond hope she was wrong, that the vision she'd seen wasn't real. Her urgency sent her flying blindly in desperation. The wind had turned chilly and flakes hovered, suspended in air, but still she sped as though by going faster she might alter the outcome.

The monotonous whish-thump of the windshield wipers kept pace with her mantra the last half hour . . . "please be wrong, please be wrong, please be wrong."

By the time she arrived at Summerset the snowflakes were sticking. The one lamp she'd left on in the living room shone through the window as the garage door closed. She raced into the house.

✦ FOURTEEN ✦

"**W**ills? Wills, are you here?"

No response, no presence.

"*Wills!*" she screamed.

"Please, Wills," she sobbed, "please, say something."

No part of her felt him. He was gone. She had sensed when his spirit left, but she wanted so desperately to have been wrong. Had he known? Would he have told her? Had he had any control over when his alteration would happen? Had he waited for her to be away?

Those were questions tormenting her mind as she collapsed to the couch, uncontrolled sobs wracking her body, cries of anguish drowning out the sound of the driving wind outside. "Wills, please, I can't do this without you."

Even the chill air sympathized and wailed its mournful lament into the dark void of silence. Weeping with a grief like none that had consumed her before lasted until she was spent and slipped into a deep, troubled sleep. In her dreams she saw him, heard him, and woke with a start, thinking his loss had only been a nightmare.

The truth of her loneliness greeted her in despondent waves as she mourned the death of a man who had been dead for generations.

She was so cold. She needed to get up, get a blanket, start a fire, turn up the thermostat, do anything to cut the bone-searing chill, but she didn't care enough. What mattered now?

Her eyes hardly blinking in their fatigue, she watched the frost outside paint ice flowers on the windows. Wills . . . he had been part of Summerset for so long. Where was he? How would she survive?

The frigid air finally motivated her from her resting place. She heard him in her heart . . . *You're a survivor! You were knocked down more times than I can remember, but you got right back up. Every time you tried again. You cried and railed at your fate, then showed 'em who's boss. You are amazingly resilient. You're my hero.* The memory of his words gave her courage as she sat where they had been together so often.

The warm droplets of water sluicing over her thawed the muscles that had become stiff with cold but did nothing for the ache in her heart. "Oh, Wills," she said, her face turned into the comforting spray of the shower, "were you aware it was time?" Torment tore through her.

How would she do this? This sorrow was different than when she'd lost Josh. There was so little love between them, but Wills consumed her being. How would she be able to stay here without him? Tears mixed with beads of water rushing toward her broken heart.

She dried herself and dressed in warm clothes, then climbed beneath the covers. She needed sweet oblivion. She couldn't think any more.

Her initial waking excitement turned instantly to

heartache the following morning when reality slammed at her core. "Wills," she whispered, but there was no answering voice, no awareness of his presence. Her breath caught, but she was afraid to cry because she feared she'd be unable to stop.

Whether she wanted to or not, she would need to install the shutters. She thought back to the discovery, the joy of being shown his long hidden treasure and the care he took of her even as he was incapable of fending for himself . . . *you've learned how to face your demons and rise above the bitterness that so easily might have swallowed you. My love for you is boundless.* Always encouraging, she would hold on to his words. They were all she had left.

Frosty air flowed around her like a blast from a deep freeze as she stepped onto the porch. Raging shards of ice cut into her exposed cheeks as she cranked the mechanism to lower the window coverings that would keep her warm this winter. The simplicity with which they hung and were secured was an engineering marvel. She was able to lift them to their hooks and fasten them to the siding with ease.

Snow was halfway up her boots as she replaced the crank and put the brass fixture back into position. This storm was going to be substantial and she would be housebound for days. Removing her gloves and footwear, Maisy lit a fire with wood cut decades before. Even the fierce icy wind wasn't able to penetrate the fitted shutters. He had given her his security, although he seemed to have sensed he wouldn't be here for winter.

Had he known it would be their last morning? Tears ran unnoticed as she put one foot in front of the other, unmindful as she went through her routine. Surely he would have said something. It was better this way, regardless of whether he had knowledge before her trip. She wouldn't have left, even though she would have been unable to hold onto him. She would have made the switch so much worse. Was he prepared?

He had told her the truth from the beginning, that he would be gone when his story was told. Willie knew of his father's existence and had his own brand of freedom. Wills had been released. Her anguish was selfish, her grief for her own loss. But she could truly rejoice in her heart that he was no longer bound to these four walls.

What did that mean? Where was he? Would she ever know? Like his presence in her life, would his certainty always be beyond her understanding? Weeks came and went, and with each passing she found healing, and thankfulness for the warmth and safety of her surroundings, much of it provided by the love of a man who'd been dead for many years. Previous winters had not been as secure as these times being cozy in the first blast of a New England winter.

She often stood in front of the mirror, searching for him. When her heart eventually accepted the reality of his absence, she was able to find a semblance of peace.

Days were filled with their own brand of quiet sorrow and joy. Her new story flew from motivated fingertips and Jonnell pronounced each page, each chapter better than the last. All the passion she'd been capable of was now channeled into a gratifying outlet, and Maisy woke most mornings with renewed stability and purpose. Wills had unveiled what had always existed within her and she refused to lose the gift, to squander what he had lovingly allowed her to discover.

The heavy snow was slowly melting in the bright December sun. When the weather permitted, she would take her ritual walk and dream her dreams. The stronger she got, the more she appreciated the encouragement she had received from her ghostly confessor.

One morning she left home to stock up on supplies, but her car had a mind and destination of its own. Several hours later she found herself sitting in front of the magnificent home she'd come to love so well.

"You are a sight for sore eyes! Come in, come in!"

The massive mahogany door must have been at least eight feet tall. When it closed behind them, she threw herself into his arms.

"He's gone, Willie." She cried for the first time in days. She couldn't tell the elderly gentleman who wrapped her in his embrace that she'd been in love with his father's ghost, his father who had been dead for seventy-plus years. But she drew comfort in his touch. They had shared a moment out of time that no one else would ever believe to be truth.

"Some mornings I wake up and question whether or not I dreamed you," he said. "You've given me a contentment in my spirit I never believed possible. I will be eternally grateful."

"It wasn't me, it was him. And I'm so glad I made the drive today. Every now and then it's the same for me and I convince myself it wasn't real, that I imagined it all, and then I remember you and know we will both be forever altered by him."

"Can you stay for lunch?"

"I'd love to, thank you."

"Betty's visiting a friend. She'll be sorry she missed

you," he said as he led them to the grand dining room, their footsteps echoing in the imposing hall. "Sit down and I'll have cook fix an extra plate."

"If you're sure it's not too much trouble."

"No trouble at all. I'll be right back."

When he returned he took the seat next to her.

They enjoyed the next hour together, sharing how the past few months had changed each of their lives.

"Tell me about when he left."

Tears came unbidden and he reached for her hand. "Take your time."

"I don't think he knew when it was going to happen. At least he didn't tell me if he did."

"Was it a shock?"

She considered how little or how much she should tell him, finally settling on middle ground.

"We had attained a breakthrough," she said. "I came home from my visit with you and I saw him standing in the room."

"Truly?"

"Yes. It was strange. He was transparent, a word he often used to describe himself." She smiled at the memory. "But I no longer needed the mirror to view his frame, to see him walking toward me."

He shook his head gently. "I'm sorry I didn't come back with you."

It was her turn to offer him comfort as she laid her hand on his. "He and I talked about that possibility. He said he didn't understand the how or why of it, but he knew you would not be able to see him."

He bowed his head. "Thank you for that."

"Before I came up here the last time, I assembled a slide presentation for him of your life. There's quite a bit of information available online of you and your family, and I put a video together in chronological order. The whole thing lasted about an hour, and three or four times he asked me to play it so he could watch you grow up again."

He pulled a handkerchief from his pocket and dabbed at his eyes and cheeks. "I'd appreciate it if you would email that to me, if you don't mind."

"Of course. I'd be honored to."

"You've given this old man new life. You're as dear to me as if you were my own granddaughter. There is no shame when I tell you I love you."

"And I love you as well. You're my family and always will be. And stop it with the 'old man.' You're still vital and vibrant."

"Spoken like a young woman with her whole life ahead of her."

They exchanged a smile and she continued. "We'd had this sensational development and I could see him. I had appointments in Augusta in a few days, but we agreed that when I came home we would work on how much further we could push the envelope, find out if we could advance to the point of actually being able to have a tactile sense of each other."

"Did you ever fear you were living in *The Twilight Zone*?"

She grinned with remembered amusement. "When he first showed himself to me, that's exactly what I said. He, of course, had no idea what I was talking about."

They were both amused at her memory.

"When I told him goodbye that morning and we made plans, he touched me and I got . . . I'm not sure how to explain it except to describe the sensation as a small electric shock. We were so excited to pursue what that meant. Nothing was any different when I left.

"He said he didn't know what would trigger his departure, but I will always believe he was unaware his leaving would happen that day. The only catalyst he understood was you finding the truth."

He hesitated. "Did he know . . . I'm not sure how to ask this. Did he know where he was going? What was waiting for him on the other side?"

Again she stroked his hand. "He had no idea. But he wasn't afraid. He was ready. He'd been held prisoner in a dungeon of loneliness for so long."

"I hope before I die I can find forgiveness in my heart for Freddy," he said. "I've thought about his lies and treachery since you were here last, and fantasized about whether or not I would have him killed if he hadn't already drunk himself to death."

"I'll tell you what Wills shared with me many times. It's *you* who is the one destroyed by holding onto the hatred. Freddy's dead. His awful deeds set the groundwork for what was to come. We can't change any of that. But we can be better from this point forward. Learn to let the bitterness go. If he taught me nothing else, that's what I learned best from your father."

"My father . . . such a strange concept to think of a young slip of a girl knowing my real father who died almost eight decades ago. It's fascinating, and every now and then I envy you."

"I wonder all the time if there are other people in the world who have had a similar experience. I'm not so vain as to think it's never happened before, but I've done a lot of research and I've never seen anyone claiming an occurrence like this as truth."

"Never once have I doubted it. Since your last visit, I

have stood in front of the wall in my closet more times than I can count, surprised each time that something was hidden there. It went unnoticed decade upon decade, its secrets locked away. You couldn't have made that up, and not another living soul had that information. I marvel at the genius of my grandfather who engineered it."

"I have a soft spot for both of your grandparents."

"I have vague recollections of my grandmother, but my overwhelming sense when I remember her is how much I loved her."

"Wills felt the same way."

"Thank you. For everything I'll never be able to express, thank you."

"Don't be silly. I've done nothing but tell a story." She got up to leave. "I'll come back and visit you both soon. The book should be in print before too long. I'll bring you a final copy when it's published."

"I'd appreciate that. No one will believe the words are anything but an intriguing fantasy. Very few of us will be aware of the truth." His seemed pleased. "I rather like that notion."

He took her in his solid embrace and held her. "Forgive my meddling, but may I ask you a question?"

"Of course," she said, still standing in the shelter of his arms.

"Were you in love with him?"

Her sob startled her, but there was no way she could have kept the heartbreak inside at his discernment. He rocked her and soothed her with gentle words. "Oh, sweet girl, how could you not have been?" he said with surprising insight. "Close quarters, similar in age, common desires, both attractive and caring and sympathetic to the other's plight."

He took a deep breath. "You may be batty, but the heart wants what the heart wants."

They broke apart in shared humor and understanding. "I promise, it's going to be all right. You will heal in time and be better for having known him. I wish I had."

She rose on her tiptoes and gave him a heartfelt kiss on his cheek. "From the bottom of my heart, thank you."

His eyes were misty, a poignant smile tugging lips that were so much like his father's. "Do you suppose there's a way I could adopt you?" He wasn't really teasing. Looking into her upturned face, he said, "You'll always have a place here in this home, and here." He put his hand over his heart. "No matter what comes or goes in life, you will always be welcome, always be a part of this family."

Her mood was buoyant as she drove back to Summerset, recognizing the closure her visit with Willie had given her.

"Hey, Jonnell, I'm going to spend Christmas with my parents and head home the day after. Do you want to have coffee on Boxing Day and catch up? Yeah, I'll deliver the rest of the manuscript I just finished. I'm anxious to get on with the next one. Ideas are churning and screaming to be released."

Her contentment was genuine as they made arrangements to meet the following week. "I *am* doing well, thank you. Feeling as healthy as I've been in a long time. Sure thing. See you then."

༼ঠ৴ঽৡ

Winter was coming to a close and the days were consistently warmer. She set an armload of groceries on the counter and thought about how she had everything she wanted – everything but him. *A Conflict of Wills* was published to rave reviews and topped the *New York Times* and *USA Today* Bestseller lists. Whenever people asked her questions about the inspiration for her book, she thought of the months she and Wills had spent together. There was a constant ache at his loss, but she refused to misuse her newfound vitality.

Her next book would be in print soon and her current novel was flowing nicely. She resumed her daily walks with the mild weather and did most of her planning and plotting while walking the bluffs overlooking Penobscot Bay. The lapping water under the frozen shell at the water's edge gave her a promise of new life. She and the world appeared to be thawing.

Standing in the doorway of the office, she admired the mirror that held a life of its own. There wasn't a day she didn't miss Wills, didn't remember their days together. When she was being fanciful she even imagined he'd saved her life, but she could hear him explain he'd only shown her the mettle she already had. They were both right.

ॡॣ

There was contentment in the act of removing the shutters that brought a tranquil joy. Wills had been gone for over six months and her heart had settled into a peaceful acceptance. Spring had arrived with new life, new beginnings. There was an appreciation for the mind that had conceived and built such a brilliant design as the shutters. Even with her slight stature she was able to maneuver them without strain.

She returned the crank and pushed the antique sconce into its clever resting place. A late-model sports car pulled into the yard, crunching the last remnants of snow and the underlying pine needles. People rarely visited. Suspicious of the unfamiliar vehicle, Maisy moved to stand at her open front door.

The lithe man who got out was as memorable to her as her own reflection.

"Wills?"

"Hi. I'm William Raines," he said, extending his hand, a charming smile lighting his face.

"How did you get here?" she asked in a whisper as she took his hand. She was disoriented, and the rush of adrenaline made her dizzy.

"I bought my uncle Jonathan's place up the street. And I drove," he teased. "Are you Margaret?"

She nodded, eyes never straying from his achingly familiar face. She studied the lines of his chin that she knew intimately, and the blue eyes that were brilliant in their regard.

"Aunt Sarah said you purchased the family mirror?"

No words left her lips as she slowly moved her head up and down.

"You bought the house from my father, Donovan Raines. I've been traveling and was out of the country for a while." They were almost eye-to-eye, she standing on the porch and he in the yard.

"Cat got your tongue?"

She wasn't even going to try to explain the craziness of her tears as she reached to take his hand again, wanting to touch him, to verify he was real. "Wills," she said again.

His reply was an expression that warmed her. "I've spent the past few days with my grandfather. You cast some sort of magic spell over him. He's fond of you, you know. Said you're an author."

"Your grandfather?" She was in a fog and couldn't put a coherent thought together.

"Yes. He said to tell you Willie sends his love." She knew that gleaming smile.

All the pieces fell into place.

"Are you William Andrew Raines?"

"Yes, named after my grandfather and my great-great uncle."

Confusion crossed her beautiful face. "No, he wasn't your uncle, he was . . ." But unless Willie had told him, he wouldn't understand, and it was too soon for anyone to be hearing such crazy tales.

"He also asked me to tell you he saved the story for you to . . . his exact words were, 'distribute at your discretion.' Said you'd know what he meant." He shook his head a little, but his grin lingered. "I've never known him to be secretive, but you seem to have bewitched him."

"We shared some memorable times, that's true."

"Whatever it was, he waxed poetic. High praise indeed."

"Thank you. The bewitching was mutual."

"How long ago did you meet each other?"

"Not long, but forever," she said vaguely.

"Well, he doesn't take kindly to most people, so you've got a champion for life."

"I appreciate that, Wills."

"Why do you call me 'Wills'?"

"It has a familiar feel. If we're going to be neighbors, it seems more casual. You don't mind, do you?"

"You mean more casual like 'Margaret'?" His laugh was ironic. "I think that's fair. I rather like 'Wills.'"

"Me too." She grinned. "There's energy to it."

"Do you go by Margaret?"

She was staring but couldn't look away. "Yes," she finally said.

"Margaret is so formal. You won't mind if I call you 'Maisy,' will you?"

She grabbed the porch rail. It was one piece of information she had purposely left out when she told Willie about his father. She was confused with this new twist, but was immune to having to make sense of the happenings at Summerset.

"Why in the world would you call me Maisy?" she asked quietly, looking for answers to so many questions.

"The common nicknames wouldn't suit you. Maisy is young and lighthearted and carefree, all descriptions my grandfather used when expounding upon your virtues."

The hair rose on her arms. "I think I like it," she said, studying the face as recognizable to her as her own. "Wills and Maisy it is." Her smile came from her soul. "What brings you out here, Wills?"

He was as enthralled as she. A soft breeze whispered through the pines and birds sang their lilting tunes. Neither heard nor were in a hurry to end this interlude.

"The mirror's been in my family for at least a century. I wondered if you'd be interested in selling it."

"That's a tricky question." Suddenly remembering her manners, she said, "Forgive me for making you stand out here. Can I fix you something to eat?"

"If you don't mind, I'd like that very much. I'm moving in and don't have groceries yet except a few cans of God-knows-what that Aunt Sarah left."

Before she reached the handle, he was beside her holding the door open. "After you." He touched her back as the screen closed behind them.

"How long will you be in Castine?" She was breathless from his touch.

"At least six months while I plan the next phase of my life. My furniture's being delivered tomorrow but it's pretty sparse."

"Because you've been traveling?"

"No, because I don't need much. I'd rather open windows and let in nature instead of cluttering my surroundings with possessions that will tie me down."

Her heart tumbled at the familiar words. "Like a mirror?" she asked softly.

His throaty laugh sent her pulses screaming. "Touché. May I see it?"

She could see him and knew he'd be standing in the room if she turned to look, tangible. The echo of long-ago whispered encouragement soothed her. *You need a flesh and blood man who can take you in his arms and love you the way you need to be loved, not a ghost who can't even dry your tears.*

"What has you smiling like the cat who swallowed the canary, Maisy?"

Their eyes met in the reflection. "I'll tell you sometime, but our imaginations need to stretch a little, and you'd run screaming for the hills if I tried to explain now." Her mouth twisted in a wry grin. "Suffice it to say I've been intimately acquainted with your family for some time and you seem familiar to me, probably because you remind me so much of your grandfather."

"Funny you should say that. Every morning when I look in the mirror, his face is staring at me. No matter where I am, he seems to be there too." His grin was wide. "I imagine that's exactly what I'll look like when I'm his age, if I'm lucky."

"Good genes, I'm sure."

"Of course," he said with a wink. His eyes roamed her face, settling on her upturned lips. "But all of his glowing words didn't do you justice."

A rosy blush crept across her cheeks.

"He talked of little else but you my entire visit," he said, stepping closer to the mirror. "That's probably why we feel as though we know each other." The material of his shirt pulled tightly across the muscles of his arms and back. Having him in front of her had her off balance. He touched the small chip in the bottom right corner.

"There's an interesting story that goes along with that imperfection," she said. "I'll tell you about it when the time's right."

"I had forgotten how beautiful it is. In truth, it belongs right here." He stepped back to admire it. "This space appears to be specially made for it. Look at that view in the reflection. No need to tote it down the street. If it's all right with you, I'll enjoy it on *your* wall every now and then."

"No doubt it's exactly where it belongs."

"Is the offer for food still open, or may I take you to lunch?" he asked. "I'm ravenous."

"Oh! Excuse my manners. Let's stay here. I've got plenty and it will be quicker. Would you like a glass of wine while I fix us something?"

"Perfect, thank you," he said, looking around as they came into her sunny kitchen. "It's remarkable how you've transformed the cottage. My memories of this place were dark and rustic. You've done an impressive job."

"Thanks. *I* like it."

She was coming out of hibernation, just like the season around her. "Why don't you tell me about your recent travels while I make lunch?"

"It's a deal. If you're interested, I could tell you about hiking in the Alps, or maybe spending an afternoon at the Acropolis in Athens. Or you could tell me about your newest book. Grandfather said I'll find it fascinating, and that it published to rave reviews."

She nodded, imagining his reaction to it.

"I hope I'm not intruding on your space. Oh! I almost forgot. He asked me to give you this." He pulled a slip of paper from his pocket and handed it to her. "Said it will make sense to you."

She sat next to him and unfolded the monogrammed linen stationery. The precise, flowing, old school handwriting read:

Child of my heart. I hope you don't mind, but I am sending THE END to you. I trust it will be all you wanted and more. If you will remember my parting words, my motives may be partially selfish. Always yours, W.A.R.

Tears sprang to her eyes as the corners of her mouth lifted.

"What is it, Maisy? Are you laughing or crying?" he asked, touching her arm.

"Yes," she said, folding the letter and slipping it into her pocket as she stood. "Yes."

She turned a dazzling smile on him. "He was right. It's no intrusion in the least for you to stop by. Make yourself at home and I'll feed you." She poured them a glass of one of her favorite wines.

"Let's start with the Acropolis and proceed from there. I look forward to hearing about your adventures over time, and, in turn, telling you ones as fascinating as any foreign location you've encountered."

THE END

If you enjoyed *Maisy's Mirror*, please consider leaving a review on Amazon, Goodreads, or both.

CURRENT BOOKS BY MIMI FOSTER

THUNDER SNOW – Contemporary
Thunder on the Mountain Book 1 – stand alone

An admired but reclusive businessman wants nothing to do with emotional entanglements. When a self-sufficient redhead invades his sanctuary, he must set aside his past to protect her from a stalker bent on destruction.

THUNDER STRUCK – Contemporary
Thunder on the Mountain Book 2 – stand alone

*Betrayed New York lawyer escapes to an isolated town. As she and a local contractor remodel a Victorian mansion, they find old journals that mirror the present as history begins repeating itself. (**MADELINE MANOR** is the non-explicit version.)*

THUNDER STORM – Contemporary
Thunder on the Mountain Book 3 – stand alone

A blaze of fascination ignites each time the zany New York ad executive and a hunky Colorado contractor meet, but neither is willing to get involved in a long distance relationship.

❧

JORDAN'S GIFT – Historical Novella
Prequel to *Thunder on the Mountain* – stand alone

A hardened mine owner has little tolerance for people until he encounters a fiery newcomer who is running from the conventions of society and a broken engagement to his archrival. He will do anything to protect her from the smooth talking, black hearted, jilted fiancé.

❧

WILLOW'S SECRET – Historical
Prequel to *Thunder on the Mountain* – stand alone

She's too busy for daydreams of handsome heroes, but a generous, well-respected railroad heir has no shame in fanning the fiery flames of attraction that spark every time he and the vibrant young woman are near each other.

❧

MAISY'S MIRROR – Contemporary
Non-series – stand alone

A young widow living in seclusion buys an antique mirror and falls in love with a handsome reflection who shares an intriguing tale of love and betrayal. Will she find the strength to convey his story to release him from his ethereal prison and from her life?

EXCERPT
THUNDER STRUCK

Mimi Foster

ONE

*A*s Andrew took my face in his hands and kissed me on the forehead, nose, and lips, there was no way I could have known that my whole world would be turned upside down by this time tomorrow.

"So I'll see you for lunch?" he asked.

"That works for me. I have a dress fitting and a few errands in the morning, but I can meet you at The James by noon."

"You sure you won't stay the night? I promise I'll make it worth your while."

"Three more weeks, then we have the rest of our lives. And I have to admit, I'm enjoying our new playfulness. How are you holding up?"

"Come home with me and I'll show you," he said, pulling me tight against him.

"You're incorrigible."

He took my face once more and gave me his special kiss. We had made the decision to not sleep together the last month before the wedding, and our relationship was benefiting from a fresh degree of flirtatiousness.

What a whirlwind it had been. With the planning and arrangements of our upcoming vows and honeymoon, and the sale of my New York co-op, I'd taken an extended leave of absence from the law firm. An associate who was out of town for a month let me sublet her apartment, and somewhere in the mix I even inherited a Bed and Breakfast in a tiny town in Colorado. I'd done research on the mountain village where it was located, and hoped to talk Andrew into a side trip during our travels. It sounded romantic.

The past few years had been twelve-hour days with little down time, so this working vacation was a coveted time to unwind. I turned my case files over to Andrew and could easily fill him in if he had questions. It sometimes surprised me that we'd been able to build a relationship, but our working proximity made it convenient and he had been persistent.

"Good evening, Jordanna." He answered the phone in his distinctive, clipped voice. "Ready to come back to work?" I loved that my father always called me by my given name.

"Not a chance, but thanks for the offer," I said affectionately. "I'm calling to let you know I've cleared my schedule and turned everything over to Andrew. I brought him up-to-date on my caseload, so if you have questions, you can check with him."

"Are you sure he's up to the task?"

"You're not?" I was slightly surprised at his question.

"Oh, don't get me wrong. He seems competent

enough, but he doesn't hold a candle to Jordanna Olivia. I trust your judgment, however, so if he's going to be my son-in-law, I'll commence showing him the inner sanctum of Whitman and Burke."

"I appreciate your vote of confidence. He's clever at handling my clients in a savvy and capable manner."

"That's never been a question, but I'll start giving him more responsibility. Don't be a stranger. Stop in when you're around. Maybe we can do lunch next week? Call Carol and set something up."

"Of course. Thank you, Father."

⁊⊙⥸

The early September air was brisk and added a degree of bounce to my step. I had a list of things I wanted to accomplish before I met Andrew for lunch. We were meeting a realtor afterwards to look at a Brooklyn Brownstone we were interested in purchasing. Finishing two errands, I was lighthearted with my newfound freedom as I entered the third store. The boutique was elegantly subdued and had been highly recommended. I wanted lingerie for our wedding night, and the garden-level provided just the right amount of light and privacy for intimate apparel shopping.

Coming out of the fitting room, I saw Andrew through the tinted window leaving the building across the street. Surprised and pleased to see him, I started to call out when I remembered my scanty attire. Hurrying to the dressing room, I grabbed my phone and headed back to the window to text him and let him know where I was. He turned just then toward the blonde woman who walked out behind him. Their lips almost touched, and I thought I was mistaken that it was Andrew, so I set down my phone.

He held her face in his hands and kissed her forehead, nose, and lips. The breath left my body. His arms embraced the fair-haired beauty who laid her head on his chest as he stroked her in the all-too-familiar way he had done to me so often. I tried to reactivate my brain to grasp what to do next.

Think, Jordan, think. Seconds passed before the adrenaline surged and I became somewhat coherent and focused. I grabbed a robe from a nearby hook and quietly opened the door. Magnifying my phone camera for a close up, I was able to capture several pictures of Andrew holding her face and kissing her before they slowly broke apart. I stepped back and let the door close, imagining it was closing on a huge part of my life.

Shocked as though hit by an electric current, I was still able to text to say something had come up and I wouldn't be able to meet, and asked him to cancel our appointment. Watching as he received the message, he immediately ran to catch up with the blonde. He put his arm around her as they walked away.

Was it possible I was mistaken? The photos told me the truth. I'd been kissed like that too many times to not understand that life as I knew it had been radically altered, and my world was going to be rocked to its foundation. It was all I could do to hold myself together. The clerk was sweet when I told her something had come up and I'd have to leave without purchasing her diaphanous creations. Alternating between disbelief and anger, I was unsure where to go, what to do. Was there protocol for something like this? The more I wandered, the angrier I got.

I wasn't aware of the miles I walked, but by the time

I found myself in front of the advertising agency of my best friend, I was ready to detonate. How do you share this information? When does the trembling stop?

"What is it? What happened?" Jeni said, coming around the desk, taking me by the shoulders.

Too angry to be coherent, I pulled my phone from my purse and showed her the pictures. I saw awareness dawn, then indignation washed over her. "I was going to make excuses, think maybe you were wrong, maybe it's his cousin, maybe it's not him, but it's Andrew, isn't it?" she asked with fire in her eyes.

Nodding, I wanted to fling something. It unnerved me that I never saw it coming. I now understood the term 'blindsided.' A thousand questions, and they all came back to, "Was this my fault?"

"Don't you *dare* go there, Jordanna Olivia Whitman! This is *his* fault! You will not share an ounce of guilt, do you hear me?"

"It's not guilt, it's self doubt and anger and disbelief and stupidity in not seeing. What if I had *married* him? And the questions keep coming. How long has it been going on? Who is she? What did he want from me? But I can't seem to get away from, *How could I have been so stupid?*"

"You had no way of knowing. I can be done for the day. Let's get out of here."

As we headed down the elevator, she said, "What are you going to tell him? Surely you're calling off the wedding?"

"There's no way I can talk to him right now. I'm seeing red. And of *course* I'm calling off the wedding. I'm just not sure where to go now that I sold my co-op. How do you avoid the gigantic spotlight that'll find you when news like this breaks?"

"You can stay at my place. You know me, I'll put a favorable spin to it."

"I wouldn't think of putting you through something like that. God, Jeni, it's going to be awful."

"Jordan! Remember the letter you got last month about a Bed and Breakfast in some obscure little town? Where was that, Wyoming? Colorado? Did you ever respond?"

"People would think I was running away."

"Who gives a rip what anyone thinks? You've got lots of time off. You get to do what you want, especially right now."

"Having a drink sounds like a good option," I suggested hopefully.

"Sounds perfect. Come on."

We drank at several bars, but somewhere along the way I lost count of how many. I *was* aware, however, that with each successive stop, the funny side of today's surprise took hold. We were relaxed and silly by the time we got back to my temporary condo.

"I mean seriously, Jeni, what were the chances I'd be standing right there, right then? Kismet."

The familiar ding of Andrew's text came through. *Sorry you couldn't make it for lunch. I was so lonely without you. Want to meet for drinks?*

Can't make it. Out with Jeni. Will be in touch. Maybe you can find something else fun to do.

Nothing's fun without you.

I couldn't even respond. What a snake. How long had he been seeing her? It didn't look as though they'd just met.

"Wanna spend the night with me, Jeni? There's an

extra room. My clothes fit you. In the morning we're either on the same page, or you'll talk me down from the cliff. Please?"

"We're diabolical plotters. Of course I will." We broke into laughter again.

"And you know what else?" I asked after a few minutes of silence. "I was excited about owning a Brownstone."

"Isn't *that* the truth? You might still want to, you just have to wait 'til the dust settles from *this* fallout before you think about taking a major step like that."

Lying on the couch a while later, she asked, "How do you feel? I'm ready to tear him limb from limb. What are *you* thinking?"

"Not a clue. The idea of going to Nederland has some appeal."

"Okay, but we don't decide anything 'til morning," Jeni said. "It's been a long day and your world derailed. We're not necessarily coherent, so let's see how you feel after a good night's sleep."

The morning dawned clear. Surprisingly, so did my brain. With Jeni's encouragement, I was warming to the idea of leaving town. "Not sure where the letter ended up in the confusion of my move, but I remember the name of the realtor that the lawyer mentioned I should contact in case I wanted to sell the place. I'll call her and get whatever details I need. In the meantime, we have to notify guests, figure out what to do with the gifts, the caterers, the travel arrangements, hotels . . . the plans."

I'd never considered myself vindictive, but I was ready to proceed. Jeni and I spent the day contacting caterers and venues and making the necessary arrangements to cancel a wedding that had been in the planning stages for months. Then we went to a print shop and waited while we had 'unvitations' printed, as Jeni was calling them. My marketing pal had done a great job designing them.

It was Saturday evening. I had a plane ticket to Denver for Monday noon. I made contact so I knew how to meet Callie Weston when I got there. I hadn't spoken with Andrew since the events of yesterday morning. What surprised me was I didn't feel sad about it. I was angry and embarrassed, but I didn't feel a loss yet. Time away would help me gain perspective. There was no part of me that felt a need to answer his calls. I returned his texts to tell him I was spending the weekend with Jeni attending to wedding matters and would contact him Monday, all of which was true. It's not like he was pining for me.

"I think it's poetic justice," Jeni said, "but I don't have as much at stake as you do. Sure you want to go through with this?"

"Telling my father will be the worst, but I'm sure he'll find a way to put the famous Wiley Riley twist on it. We both know how adept he is at that sort of thing."

"No question, he's the master. Okay, sweetheart, let's get these addressed."

⸜⸝

Everything was in place by early Monday. Arrangements had been canceled and the unvites were ready for Jeni to drop in the mail. She was a trooper, staying with me the whole time, talking me through the ups and downs, helping me get the details done. Most important had been her encouragement that life was going to be deliciously different soon. I had one last stop to make before my flight.

Knowing he was at work, I used my key to let myself into Andrew's apartment. My purpose was twofold: to make sure I had all my belongings from his place, and to leave him a copy of the unvite so he'd have a clue of what was about to hit him.

Jeni and I discussed the pros and cons of giving him warning, but it was all the more appealing to think he would know beforehand and there wouldn't be a thing he could do to stop it. I had momentary twinges of doubt about whether or not to go through with it until I saw two wine glasses in the sink, one with a lipstick imprint. I had made the right decision. Much harder would be the phone call to my father during the cab ride.

As Jordan was landing at Denver International Airport, Andrew was arriving home after a tiring day. They hadn't spoken in a while, but he recognized her handwriting on the distinctive envelope on the counter. He immediately looked around, hoping nothing was out of place, and made a mental note to remember to be more careful in the future.

It was strange that her key was on the counter. "Jordan?" he called out. "You here?" He let out a sigh of relief as he reassured himself everything appeared to be in order - until he picked up the letter and noticed it was propped against two wine glasses, one with the betrayal of red lipstick on its rim. Tearing open the envelope, he saw the bold, perfect lettering that proclaimed: *LOVE IS BLIND*. He fell into a chair as he opened the card to see an intimate picture of him kissing Mary Ann with large letters announcing: *FORTUNATELY, I'M NOT*.

If you've enjoyed reading any of these books, please consider leaving a review on Amazon or Goodreads. And I love to hear from readers, so drop me a line at mimi@mimifoster.com or follow me on my website MimiFosterBooks.com.

ABOUT THE AUTHOR

Bestselling writer of steamy romance novels in the early morning hours, award-winning Realtor during the day, Mimi is an incurable romantic who loves to create sexy but tender escapes about unforeseen encounters that forever alter lives for the better.

In addition to being married to her perfect human, Mimi is a blogger and photographer. She made five perfect female humans (her greatest achievement). They, in turn, have made five more small perfect humans.

She loves to hear from readers, so be sure to find her on her website (MimiFosterBooks.com), or interact with her on social media.